The Pilates Class

By

Stevie Turner

Synopsis

The Pilates Class is a quick read, and a humorous look at the lives and loves of several different characters attending a Pilates exercise class for the first time.

Roger is a down-to-earth builder type, Judy is the harassed single mother of four teenage boys, and Thelma is a librarian who usually looks as though she's been sitting on a wasps' nest for most of her life. Neville is on the lookout for a woman (any woman will do), and Julian just wants to be young again. Edie is the wrong side of 70, and Roz is a size zero fitness queen.

These characters, together with one very overweight Alice, all meet up for the first time at their local Pilates class. Petra, the class instructor, has no idea what she has let herself in for!

Table of Contents

CHAPTER 1 1
CHAPTER 2 5
CHAPTER 3 9
CHAPTER 4 13
CHAPTER 5 15
CHAPTER 6 19
CHAPTER 7 23
CHAPTER 8 27
CHAPTER 9 33
CHAPTER 10 37
CHAPTER 11 41
CHAPTER 12 47
CHAPTER 13 53
CHAPTER 14 57
CHAPTER 15 59
CHAPTER 16 63
CHAPTER 17 69
CHAPTER 18 73
CHAPTER 19 79
CHAPTER 20 81
CHAPTER 21 85
CHAPTER 22 89
CHAPTER 23 91
CHAPTER 24 93
CHAPTER 25 97
CHAPTER 26 101
CHAPTER 27 105
CHAPTER 28 109
CHAPTER 29 113
CHAPTER 30 115
CHAPTER 31 119
CHAPTER 32 123
CHAPTER 33 127

CHAPTER 34.. 129
CHAPTER 35.. 133
CHAPTER 36.. 137
CHAPTER 37.. 141
CHAPTER 38.. 145
CHAPTER 39.. 149
CHAPTER 40.. 153
CHAPTER 41.. 157
CHAPTER 42.. 161
CHAPTER 43.. 165
CHAPTER 44.. 171
CHAPTER 45.. 175
CHAPTER 46.. 179
CHAPTER 47.. 181
EPILOGUE 183

CHAPTER 1

ROGER HARVEY COULD taste blood. He had bitten the inside of his mouth to stop himself from screaming.

"How was the injection for you?"

"Bloody awful. The pain's worse now, doc."

Roger rubbed his aching shoulder and tried not to panic on finding that he could no longer raise his arm at all.

"The pain will ease after a few days as the steroid works its way in. You'll need to keep the joint moving, or the injection will be of no use. Start by moving the fingers of the affected arm upwards along a wall every day and see how far you can reach. Make another appointment to see me if there's no improvement after a couple of weeks."

"Thanks doc."

"Blimey Dad – you look a bit white!" Lewis stood up as he saw his father gingerly walking out of the consultation room.

"So would you if you'd just had a foot long needle shoved into your shoulder joint."

"Ewwww…..that sucks."

"Yeah."

"I told Mum where I was taking you today, and Barry said

he had the same thing a while back. He joined something called a plates class at the leisure centre, and said it really helped."

"The wonderful Barry can go fuck himself and mind his own business. Come on; get me out of here."

Lewis manoeuvred the van down the exit ramp of the hospital car park, and joined the rush hour traffic along the main road out of Norwich.

"When shall I tell Bill that you'll be back at work then?"

"I'll go back on Monday. I'm going to the GP later on to get a certificate for the rest of the week."

"We'll be starting on the footings for that new housing estate."

"Yeah. I'll be there."

"Sure you'll be all right Dad?" Lewis swung the van into Meadow Close and turned off the engine. "Want me to come up?"

"No, you get off home. Thanks for the lift. I'll see you on Monday."

Roger turned the key in the lock of his one bedroom second floor flat, and gave a rueful laugh. Two years ago before the divorce it was a detached house with three bedrooms. Amanda had worked it all out to her advantage.

He sank down on the bed and closed his eyes. The pain was intense in his shoulder, making him irritable and bad tempered. Thank God he could raise his arm up a bit more now though. For a moment there he thought he was buggered.

He must have dozed off. Waking suddenly and glancing at his mobile phone, a reminder was showing for his GP appointment in half an hour. Roger leapt off the bed, and ignored protesting stabs of pain from his newly injected shoulder joint. There was just enough time for a quick cup of coffee; the doctors' appointments usually ran late anyway.

"I'll sign you off until Monday. Keep the joint moving and keep stretching the arm. Do you belong to a gym?" Having taken a quick look at the burgeoning beer belly on the patient, Dr Khan thought he already knew the answer to that question.

"No."

Surprise. Surprise. "I'll give you a 6 week gym prescription." The doctor handed Roger a piece of paper. "Give this to the manager of your local leisure centre. Your best bet is a Pilates class that will help stretch and tone your muscles. You'll be amazed at the results if you stick to it."

Roger sniffed as he took the piece of paper. If Dr Khan thought that he, Roger, was going to prance about in leggings and a stretchy leotard with a load of skinny women, then he could fuck right off.

"Is it going to cost me anything?"

"No. It's free for six weeks. After that you can decide whether or not you want to carry on with it."

Well, if it's free then it might be worth having a go? Who knows? Perhaps one of those skinny women might even fancy him in his leotard......

CHAPTER 2

"BRIAN, I ASKED you to look after Elliott! Where is he?" Judy Barr put down the groceries on the kitchen table and took off her coat.

"He said he was going to the park with his mates. When's dinner?"

"You know what goes on at the park. When I'm late home from work you have to keep an eye on him."

"Mum, be serious. Who's going to nick him? He weighs fourteen stones for God's sake!" Brian looked in the grocery bags. "Did you buy any crisps?"

"No, money's a bit tight this month. It's not about him being abducted; I worry about the drinking and the drug taking down there. I worry that he'll get in with the wrong crowd."

"All Elliott and his mates do is sit on the swings and eat takeaway pizzas and chips. Nick's down there snogging in the bushes with his bird. He'll see what he's up to."

Judy sighed and began preparing the evening meal. Life had dealt her a rough hand: Alan was living it up in Bromley with Cara, discarding his responsibilities like a snake shedding its outer skin, and thinking all he had to do was to pay the least amount of money into her bank account from afar that he could get away with. How was she supposed to earn a living and look after the welfare of four teenage boys at the same time?

"Is dinner ready yet, Mum?" Marlon had appeared from the fug of his bedroom.

"Not yet. Have you done your homework?"

"We weren't set any."

"You said that yesterday."

"We weren't set any yesterday either. What's for dinner?"

"Spaghetti Bolognese."

"I hate spaghetti Bolognese."

"Then cook me something lovely then. I could do with a night off."

"No, it's ok. I'll eat it. It just tastes like shit."

"Please watch your language Marlon."

"I can't think of any other word to describe it."

As if by magic all four boys appeared in the kitchen just as Judy was draining the spaghetti. Their appetites were insatiable; her weekly food bill was rising faster than the national debt. She decided after dinner to ask Alan for more money.

"Cara wants a new kitchen. We'll have to be a bit careful with the pennies, Jude."

You have four ravenous sons here. You are bloody well going to pay for their upkeep.

"All I'm asking for is another fifty pounds a month to help with the food bill."

"What's Brian doing these days?"

If you were any sort of decent father you would know.

"He's in the first year of his engineering apprenticeship. He's doing ok but he's earning the usual peanuts."

"Make it thirty five quid and it's a deal."

"Forty five. Elliot's comfort eating; he misses his Dad. It's like trying to feed a plague of locusts."

"Forty." Alan appeared totally insensitive to his youngest son's plight.

"Ok. Forty." Judy thought it was best not to press for

more; she was lucky he had even agreed to forty pounds.

"How much did the bastard give you?" Nicholas picked up a tea towel and laconically dried a few plates.

"Thank you for helping me wash up, Nick. Your father's given another forty pounds a month."

"Well, that should keep Elliott in pizzas anyway."

"I'm going to have to give him less pocket money and put him on a diet. He's not going to like it, but I've been a bit lax with him lately. He misses his Dad. He's suffered a bit more than the rest of you."

"I'll take him down the pub with me and give him a few games of snooker."

"That's really kind of you!" Judy turned towards her son; "Is that aftershave I can smell? It's a nice pong. What's her name?"

"Er……..Tracey. She lives in Detmar Road."

"She's definitely bringing out the best in you!" Judy smiled and rinsed out the washing up bowl.

As she settled down in bed, she could hear Marlon's music vibrating through the whole house. The 'singer' (if that's what they called singing these days) sounded angry; the tor-rent of expletives being shouted through the thin walls was enough to make a sailor blush. Sighing, she climbed out from under the warm duvet, only to find that Brian was out on the landing already.

"Turn it down, you wanker!"

Peace suddenly reigned. Brian's booming bass tones seemed to have done the job for her. As she got back under the covers she decided that she really wanted to attend some sort of relaxation class. Perhaps it would make her less prone to worrying all the time? She would check at the leisure centre after work tomorrow and find out what they had on offer.

CHAPTER 3

"HAVE YOU GOT that 'Fifty Shades' book?"

Thelma Frost looked at the little old lady standing opposite. Her head barely reached above the counter top.

"It's out on loan I'm afraid, but I'll put your name on the waiting list."

Thelma sighed. The world was obsessed with sex. She was sick of the constant sexual innuendos from the lonely old men who spent all day supposedly reading in the library. One of them she'd caught holding a mirror and bending down next to a young girl in a short skirt standing there unaware in the fiction section. Every time you opened a newspaper or magazine there was somebody's breasts looking at you. Sex was everywhere. It was on more and more TV programmes, and especially rife on the music channels. You couldn't even look at a music video these days without the unpleasant sight of half-naked women gyrating provocatively about. Why don't they just take all their clothes off and fornicate and get it over with?

"Shall I do the shelving?" Monica's voice brought Thelma out of her reverie.

"Yes, thank you Monica. I'm going for some lunch now."

Thelma took her packet of sandwiches and flask of tea out of her locker, and walked towards her usual seat in the park next to the library. She experienced a slight twinge of irritation at the sight of a young couple kissing and cuddling on her seat, and had to backtrack to the empty bench near the public toilets. A smell of stale urine wafted out from the men's lavatory. Thelma clicked her tongue in annoyance and moved off again to the other end of the small park. At this rate her lunch half hour would be over before she'd even had a chance to eat anything.

As she savoured her mother's salmon and cucumber sandwiches left over from the Sunday teatime visit of her elderly aunt and uncle, she surreptitiously watched the young couple kissing on her seat. She gave a tut of disapproval; they should be doing that sort of thing in private. She carried on watching, dark sunglasses hiding her line of vision. She could see the boy had his tongue in the girl's mouth. She looked away to pour some hot tea from her flask, and felt a fleeting sensation of something unknown in her nether regions. By the time she had put the cup to her lips the couple were walking away, arms around each other.

The afternoon shift dragged on. As Thelma stooped over to pick up some books from the bottom shelf of the returns trolley, the muscles in her lower back sent out a painful stab of protest. She stood up gingerly, holding the small of her back with her right hand and some non-fiction books in the other.

The pain was happening more and more. She knew she was out of condition. She needed to find out about joining an exercise class of some sort before her back gave up the ghost altogether.

"Is that you, Thelma?" Her mother's voice sounded as soon as Thelma returned home and put the key in the lock.

Who else would it be? The Queen of Sheba?

"Yes it's me, Mum."

"What?"

"It's me."

"You're twenty minutes' late. Your dinner's cold now." Sylvia Frost's mouth was forming a tight 'o' of disapproval as Thelma entered the kitchen.

"Sorry, Mum. I went to the leisure centre to see if there were any classes I could join that would help my bad back. The receptionist said there's a new Pilates course starting next Monday evening."

"What?"

Thelma closed her eyes for a second and let another stab of annoyance pass.

"I said there's a new Pilates course starting next Monday evening."

"You're joining the gym?"

"No. Just a Pilates class. Apparently it tones up your muscles a treat."

Thelma put her dinner in the microwave to heat up.

"So you'll be out now every Monday night?" Sylvia's voice took on the whine that Thelma knew only too well. She waited for the start of the emotional blackmail.

"I sit here all day on my own, and nobody comes near nor by."

Yep. There it was. There'll be the bit about putting her head in the oven next.

"Sometimes I feel like putting my head in the microwave."

That was a change from the oven. Wouldn't gassing be a better way to go? Just place a pillow in the oven, put your head on it, turn on the gas and close the kitchen door…

"I'll only be gone a couple of hours. It's not like I'm flying to the moon. Why not join something yourself? An evening class perhaps?"

"What?"

"How about joining an evening class?" *How am I going to get there?*

"How can I get to an evening class? I'm too old to get on the bus to the college."

No you're not. It's just that Dad drove you around everywhere when he was alive, and you became dependent and lazy. You're only 68. For God's sake get a life and stop complaining!

"I'll take you in the car. It'll be good for you to meet new people."

"No, no. I could never go anywhere on my own."

CHAPTER 4

"HOW'S THAT FOR you Mrs Lambert?"

Julian Swann held the mirror at the back of the old lady's head. He had tried his best, but every week she still seemed to resemble a rather large cauliflower.

"Lovely thanks, Julian. I'll make another appointment for a fortnight."

Julian massaged his shoulder and winced. Holding the hairdryer was becoming more and more of a problem, and he couldn't seem to lift his left arm up as high as he used to. His back ached from standing up all day. Grey hairs were beginning to appear. What was happening to his body? He was only 42! He thought back to the conversation he'd had with his partner that very morning. It was fine for Malcolm to take the piss; he was only 28 and all his body parts were working as they should. However, Julian knew the score – there could be no ageing in the gay world! What was he going to do, now that his body was no longer young?

"What's it going to be today then Mrs Cooper?"

"I don't know. What do you think?"

Julian looked at the tired, lank, over-bleached rats' tails in front of him, and thought maybe a good going over with the clippers set at 0.5 would be the best solution.

"Let's have a little trim, some hot oil conditioner and a blow dry. What do you say?"

"Sounds lovely. You always do a good job, Julian. I love your new hair colour by the way."

"Oh, thank you! I've been feeling a little bit sad these past few days, so blue is definitely the right colour at the moment."

"Nothing too serious I hope?"

"Just a painful back and shoulder. Nothing that turning back the clock by 20 years wouldn't put right."

"Ha! If only! When I had a frozen shoulder I went to some classes where they taught you how to stretch properly. Perhaps go along and see if there's anything suitable in the leisure centre?"

"Thanks. I might just do that."

"You're out of condition. You even drive to the salon. You could walk it in fifteen minutes." Malcolm gripped his right foot and pressed the heel of his trainer into his right buttock. "Come out running with me. You'll soon feel the benefit."

"It'd kill me." Julian watched as Malcolm switched to stretching his left quadriceps. He resembled a Greek God, standing there in his purple running shorts and vest: "There's no way I could get my foot right up there anyway."

"I'll come to the gym with you if you want? Anything you want to do. You can get fit slowly. We can work out together."

"You'd do that for me?"

"Only if I can have a free haircut at the salon."

"It's a deal. You're in need of a cut and colour anyway."

"Just don't do it pink like the last time. The grunters at the gym were pissing themselves."

CHAPTER 5

EDITH LAMBERT SIGHED and looked in the mirror. It was bad enough being invisible, but now Julian had styled her hair just like a cauliflower again. She wanted it to look the way it had been when she first met Leonard, when she used to walk into a room and heads would turn. However, as that had been 54 years ago she was rapidly resigning herself to the fact that it was perhaps rather optimistic to expect Julian to perform miracles, and that she would have to get used to looking not unlike a vegetable from the brassica family.

Bette Davis was right when she'd said that old age was not for sissies. Edith hated being old. Everything ached that was still working, and what didn't ache didn't work at all. Leonard was gone and her three children had moved to London as soon as they were able to look for work. Her only joy was when they visited for the day and brought the grandchildren. Edith had only ever lived in Norfolk all her life, and she was too old now to want to change her ways.

But hey, there was always a walk in the park to lift her spirits, and she could change her library book at the same time. Edith put on her coat and grabbed her bag. If she kept moving it seemed to help her backache.

The young thin-faced woman at the counter always looked as if she had never laughed in her life. Edith handed over her library book.

"That's 10 pence please Mrs Lambert. It's overdue."

"Your assistant extended it for me over the phone, dear. I forgot to write the new date in."

Thelma's face froze into a grimace as she double-checked on the computer screen. Monica had not entered any extended date in the computer. Why did they always come out with the same excuse? Was there a group leader that phoned all the other old ladies and told them what to say to avoid paying overdue fines?

"Please remember to write the date down next time."

"Have you got that Fifty Shades book?" Edith wanted to lose herself in a good racy read and forget all about her aches and pains. She couldn't have sex anymore, but could still remember what went where and what it felt like when it got there.

"I'll put your name on the waiting list." Oh God, not another one.

Edith meandered along the fiction aisles and stopped at the L – M section. She would have to make do with Lady Chatterley's Lover again. Oh good, it was still on the shelf. The young of today didn't know what they were missing!

As she made her way back to the counter a poster on the wall in front of her advertising Pilates sessions for beginners caught her myopic eye. Moving in closer she could see that all ages were welcome, and that it would be particularly good for toning muscles and helping to relieve aches and pains. Mats and gym balls would be provided free of charge.

As Edith woke up each morning wondering what was going to ache that day, she suddenly decided it was about time she started doing some exercises to help herself. She felt sure the GP was heartily sick of the sight of her; all he ever told her each time was to lose weight and do some exercise. Perhaps with Pilates the muscles around her abdomen would become so strong and toned that her waist circumference would shrink by 10 inches? Ha! Pigs might fly!

The doorbell rang just as Betty Richards had plumped herself down with her coffee and digestive biscuit to watch the Jeremy Kyle show. Slightly irritated at having to get up again, she touched the pause button on the remote control and padded to the front door:

"It's only me, dear!"

"Oh, come in Edie. I've just made some coffee. Would you like a cup? Your hair looks nice."

"Lovely!" Edith patted a stray white lock into place. "Julian did it this morning. You feel better when your hair's been done don't you?"

"You do indeed. He's doing mine tomorrow. I told him I want something different this time."

"Different? Like what?"

"I want a new me. New colour; new style."

"Can't wait to see it! Talking of a new you, do you fancy coming with me to the leisure centre next Monday to try out the Pilates class for beginners?" Edith sipped her coffee. "Apparently it can help to get rid of your aches and pains."

"Look at the size of me!" Betty took another biscuit. "I'm too old and fat for anything like that."

"You're younger than me, dear. It'll be a bit of a laugh. You know, take us out of ourselves. I don't think you have to run around. It's all done on a mat that'll be provided."

"Oh, I don't know……" Betty had a sudden vision of anorexic women in skin-tight leotards and rainbow coloured leg warmers prancing about to something by the Bee Gees.

"I'll knock for you on Monday evening at 7 o'clock." Edith finished her coffee. "Put Jeremy back on."

CHAPTER 6

THERE MUST BE another way to meet women. Neville Peters had tried them all; singles' clubs, speed dating, Internet dating, chat rooms; the list was varied and endless. The women were fearsome and frustrated, and Neville was cowed. He wanted to keep his penis to himself until he got to know a woman better. Also, wasn't a man expected to make the first move? These women were virtually tearing at his trousers even on the first date. Trying a different tack he'd even once decided to learn ballroom dancing, but the ladies there, nice though they were, all appeared at least 30 years' older than himself. Still, at least he could now perform a mean Foxtrot, and you never knew when that might come in handy.

Wasn't he good-looking enough? Why were all his mates married with children and he was still single and a virgin at 38? Was he too picky? For the life of him Neville did not know. His mother's words of encouragement that somewhere there was a girl just right for him were beginning to wear rather thin. He had his own house and was making enough money as an accountant and financial advisor to be able to give the right girl a good life; it was just that Miss Right seemed to be giving him as wide a berth as she could.

Locking up the office that evening he thought ahead to his date with Kimberley. Would she finally be the one he wanted to spend the rest of his life with? The dating agency seemed to think they were made for each other.

Showered and shaved and wearing his best suit and tie, Neville sat quietly hopeful in the bar adjacent to the leisure centre, sipped a cold beer, and waited for his perfect woman to appear. He hated first dates; he hated making small talk. His eyes strayed to the entrance door every time it opened to see if any lady came in wearing a blue dress. Above the door he could also see a large poster advertising Pilates classes on Monday evenings. He sucked his stomach in. Was he getting a bit flabby? He still only weighed eleven and a half stones. Perhaps his gut was expanding? Was that putting the women off? If this one didn't turn out to be any good, then perhaps it was time to start exercising.

Neville looked again as the door to the bar opened. Yes, the lady was wearing a blue dress (if you could call it that) but probably it would have been more pleasing on the eye if the manufacturers had managed to use sufficient material to modestly cover her enormous pink arms and heaving cleavage. The dress seemed to finish just below the hips, and the ensemble was completed with a pair of black leggings stretched to breaking point over two thighs as wide as ancient tree trunks. A pair of flip-flops came slopping in Neville's direction.

"Hi! Are you Neville? I'm Kimberley, and I'm parched!"

Kimberley plopped herself down on the bar stool next to Neville. His heart sank. She had to weigh at least 18 stones. Why did the agency say that her build was small?

"Yes, I'm Neville; pleased to meet you. Would you like a drink?"

"You bet. WKD please, and have they got any crisps?"

"Do you live around here, Nev?" Kimberley had finished the drink and bag of crisps in record time.

CHAPTER 7

"SLOW DOWN JIMMY! Mummy can't run that fast!" Roz Ellis kept an eye on her son as he cycled along the footpath towards the school. She had jogged past the usual group of mothers walking along with their children, and wondered what they were going to say about her behind her back today. She didn't even know them but she knew they hated her. Anyway, she didn't give a shit; she was leaner and fitter than all of them. She looked after her body, which was more than could be said for those gossiping bitches!

Sweating in her tight Lycra and panting slightly, she followed Jimmy round to the cycle shed.

"Don't forget to lock it up."

"Ok Mum. See you later!" Jimmy gave his mother a kiss and ran off to join a game of tag in the playground.

By the time she was jogging back out through the school gates, the other mothers were walking in. She looked in their direction, but as normal nobody even looked at her or acknowledged her presence. Roz mentally stuck two fingers up as she started to jog home; there would just be enough time to shower and change before driving to her aerobics class at the leisure centre.

"Morning Roz! Which class is it today then?" Ann, the Receptionist, looked with envy at the toned, slim woman standing in front of her.

"Hi Ann! It's aerobics this morning. I've got nothing for Mondays any more though, as the static cycling sessions closed due to lack of interest."

"We have Pilates starting on Monday evenings now. Do you want to have a go at that?" Ann wondered where the woman got her energy.

"Sure! Put me down on the list. What time?"

"7pm."

"Great. Mark will be home by then to look after Jimmy."

Freshly showered and back in her kitchen after a good workout, Roz carefully chewed her tofu, spinach and bean sprout salad. She was ravenously hungry and felt as though she could finish off the entire contents of her fridge, but with a bit of luck (if she ate slowly enough) her stomach might register its fullness before she needed to start on the big pot of fat-free natural yoghurt in the fridge door.

She hated that post-lunch dip. No matter what she ate she always felt heavy and sleepy around 2pm. She set her stop-watch and allowed herself a quick 10-minute power nap on the sofa before lacing up her trainers for a brisk walk back to the school.

"Not running this afternoon then?" There they were again in the playground; the ghastly group of gossiping over-weight mothers waiting for their equally ghastly and over-weight progeny. Roz hated this time of day.

"I've just eaten a big bowl of tofu and bean sprouts, and you can't run on a full stomach unfortunately." Roz smiled, held her head up high, and prayed that Jimmy would be the first one to run out.

"Rather you than me! Give me a pizza any day!" One of the women cackled, which set off the remainder of the group.

"A big 12 inch, eh, Alice!"

"Yeah, and a pizza!"

Roz forced a thin smile and mentally willed Jimmy to appear.

"Hi Mum! I'll just go and get my bike." Roz followed Jimmy around to the cycle sheds, glad of an excuse to get away.

"Did you eat everything in your lunch box today?"

"I swapped the hummus wrap and rice cake for some chocolate, but then Paul wanted the chocolate back but it was too late because I'd eaten it. Now Paul says he's not my friend anymore."

"You know we don't eat chocolate! It's poison! It contains over 300 chemicals. It'll make you fat and spotty like Steven."

"But it tastes nice, Mum. Why can't we eat the same food as everybody else?"

Roz sighed. She hated losing control over the food her son ate. Since starting school he had discovered crisps, cake, sweets and chocolate. The ghastly mothers had no idea of the damage they were doing to their children' s arteries. Jim-my's class teacher had even called her in after school the day before to inform her that he had been caught stealing sweets from other people's lunch boxes. She would have to have a word with Mark that evening after Jimmy was in bed.

"Give him a piece of cake in his lunch box, Roz. It's not going to kill him."

Mark could understand Jimmy's preference for saturated fat; he himself was becoming sick of mung bean stew, cous cous, quinoa and raw vegetables. He never knew his digestive system could produce so much savage flatulence. He craved white bread, chips, sausages and bacon. He had started finding excuses to visit his mother on Friday nights, knowing there would always be a massive fry-up waiting for him.

"Well, you're not much help!"

Roz could not understand her partner's aversion to healthy eating and exercise. He had been keen enough on her cooking when they had first met, and now she more than suspected he was sneaking into the transport café most mornings for bacon torpedoes.

Her little world was falling apart around her.

CHAPTER 8

"THERE'S A DISCOUNT if you pay for all 10 classes up front." However, looking at the pregnant male standing in front of her, Ann had already guessed that she was on a hiding to nothing.

"The Quack gave me 6 free classes darling, but I'll see how it goes." Roger handed over the voucher and eyed the receptionist up and down.

I'm not your darling!

"That's fine. I'll book you in for six weeks then. If you go into the gym, the Pilates room is up the stairs and first on your left.

Roger was tired. His first day back at work had been difficult. His right arm hadn't seemed to want to obey his commands, and he could only lift it to shoulder height. The pain in his shoulder had subsided somewhat since the injection, but the joint was stiff and inflexible. As he climbed the stairs he hoped that he would be able to perform most of the exercises lying down on the mat. On entering the room he was happy to see a lithe blonde of about 35 and clad in pink Lycra coming towards him.

"Good evening! I'm Petra. Find yourself a mat and sit down. We usually perform Pilates barefooted, so feel free to take your socks and shoes off. What's your name?"

"Roger, but take it from me darling that you wouldn't

want me to take my boots off. I've just come from a building site. These boots have been on for 12 hours, and it's been a hot day."

He lowered himself down stiffly, and thought he heard the woman on the mat nearest to him stifle a giggle. He looked to his left and saw a woman obviously in her forties, with short brown hair and wearing a grey tracksuit.

"Evening, darling. I'm Roger."

"Judy."

I'm not your darling!

"Pleased to meet you."

Roger looked to his right and saw a thin-faced sour looking woman wearing black leggings and a loose t-shirt, glancing over at him and wrinkling her nose in disgust. He nodded in her direction.

"Evening."

There was no reply. He tried to sit cross-legged, but it was difficult while still wearing his thick jeans and heavy steel-capped work boots. He stretched his legs out and watched Petra as she greeted what he thought were two obvious poof-tahs taking their places on the empty mats in the front row. One of them sported a blue ponytail, and the other one's hair stuck up in short purple spikes. Good God, they wouldn't last five minutes on the building site!

"Welcome, Julian and Malcolm. I'm sure we'll all get to know each other as the weeks progress."

Looking over his shoulder, Roger noticed a banker-type wearing black jogging trousers and a Rolling Stones t-shirt who definitely looked as though he was up his own arse (yes, he definitely was a merchant banker), and an old lady at the back with a cauliflower hair-do sitting as uncomfortably as himself on her mat. He could see two white and veined low-er legs sticking out from beneath a pair of three-quarter length trousers. The soles of her feet were thickened with hard skin. She flashed him a smile showing two rows of per-fect white false teeth.

"Hello darling, all right?"

"Yes thank you, dear." Edith hadn't been called darling in a long while. It made a change, even if he did seem to be a rather uncouth-looking builder. She preferred the look of the business-type man sitting alongside her on his mat, but as of yet he had not spoken a word.

"Are we ready to start? Oh, hello." Petra acknowledged the late arrival, toned and clad in tiny Lycra shorts and matching top.

"Sorry I'm late! I'm Roz."

"Welcome Roz. Take a mat. I think we're now ready to begin."

Roger looked at the vision of loveliness that had just walked in the door, and sat up straighter on his mat. Now that was classy! No wedding ring either.

Neville, crouched and silent on his mat, followed the newcomer with his eyes as she crossed her ankles and sat down on a mat at the front without using any hands for support. Hmm… good muscle control.

"Has anybody done any Pilates before? No? Ok then, we'll start with some basic stretching and core strengthening tonight, and then add in some more advanced moves another time. You'll be able to practise these at home during the week. Let's have you all standing up on your mats first of all." Petra put a CD on to play, which to Roger sounded like whales mating.

Roz bounced back up into a standing position, eager to begin. Edith and Roger took their time, lagging behind the others.

"Place your feet hip distance apart, pull your navel into your back, and let's have those arms in the air. Big breath in, then exhale and stretch up; stretch up to the ceiling!"

Julian winced and found he could only raise his left arm to just above shoulder height. How he could make his navel touch his back he had no idea. Petra noticed that Roger seemed to have a similar problem as Julian, but on the opposite side.

"I see we have two with frozen shoulders. Well, with regular stretching you will be able to improve this." Petra hoped she sounded confident enough. "Now, big breath in, and then let's exhale slowly as we bring the arms down."

There was a collective sigh.

"Breathe in, and then exhale as you lift those arms again. Come on – up they go!"

What was all this breathing to do with it? What was that bloody awful music? Roger couldn't remember if he had to breathe out or breathe in. Shit. He'd just breathe normally. He couldn't be bothered with all that malarkey. What was that bit about the navel?

"Big breath in, and then exhale slowly as you bring the arms down."

So far, so good. Edith could keep up. What a pity Betty had chickened out.

"Now, we're going to shake out those shoulders. Move them up, round and down, and up, round and down; first one way, and then the other. Lovely. Give them a good shake!" Petra thought that maybe the next exercise might start to bite a bit more and sort out the wheat from the chaff.

"Now we're going to roll down slowly, one vertebra at a time. Feet hip distance apart, toes pointing forward, and take it slowly. Keep the navel pulled in and the pelvic floor pulled up. This will stretch out the lower back. Let the arms and head hang down. Keep a little bit of a bend on the knees."

Roger wondered where the pelvic floor was. Roz had kept pace and rolled down with Petra, and Roger had a wonderful view of her small perfectly formed arse as it tilted up in the air. From between her shins Roz could see fat Roger still standing up and ogling her backside, and the one in the Rolling Stones t-shirt taking a quick look before he rolled down. At least the slimmer one is a bit subtler about it. She made a mental note to sit on one of the mats behind them the following week.

From her upside-down peripheral vision Judy could see Roger trying to bend in the middle. However, the manoeuvre seemed to be causing him some difficulty.

"You're joking Missis! I've just had a burger and chips and it ain't happening!" Roger stood upright again, his face red and sweating. Once again Judy suppressed the urge to giggle.

"Cut it out next week then and have a salad." Thelma, bent over double, turned her head to the left and looked up at Roger. She hated men like him.

"Cheers, darling." Stuck up bitch!

"Don't worry. I can't do it either. I've just had a steak and kidney pudding." Edith gave Roger another flash of her pearly white teeth.

"Come up slowly, one vertebra at a time." Petra straightened up, sighed and looked towards the back. How could you do an hour of Pilates after just eating a plateful of steak and kidney pudding? "Next week we must remember to eat only a small meal at least two hours before."

"I'm still working at 5 o'clock." Julian looked at Malcolm. "I don't want to eat that early." Malcolm put a hand through his hair. Fucking purple spikes! He'd kill Julian this time, he really would! He now looked as though he should be attending a heavy metal music festival.

"Have a big lunch then, and eat afterwards." Petra thought this would have all been common sense. It just goes to show how thick some people are!

"Let's stand with feet hip distance apart, and bring the right hand around to hug the left shoulder. Place your left hand on your right elbow, and turn your head to the left. This will stretch out the right shoulder. Count to 30 and then do the same for the right shoulder."

Roger had a quick look at Judy's back as she stretched her right shoulder. Nice figure. That stuck up bitch on the other side thought she was better than anyone else.

Thelma felt Roger's eyes burning into her back as she stretched her left shoulder. What a ghastly man he was! She made a mental note to stay at the back of the class the following week.

"Now we're going to stretch those hamstrings." Petra positioned herself on the mat. "Feet hip distance apart. Bend forward and place your hands down on the mat in front of you. Walk forward with your hands as far as you can, and keep your heels touching the floor. Keep the navel and pelvic floor pulled in. The heels must not lift up on the mat."

Jesus Christ! She must be joking! And what the fuck is the pelvic floor? Roger remained upright and watched Roz's arse. Edith watched Roz and felt a pang of jealousy. Oh to be fifty years younger and not be invisible any more! Even Julian hadn't recognised her yet. Oh to be able to attract the attention of both that builder and the banker-type! Roz obviously didn't realise what was going on in the back half of the room.......

"From that position move down onto all fours and sit back on your heels. Bend forward with your arms outstretched and the object of this exercise is to get your forehead to touch the floor."

You'll be lucky! Roger could just about manage to sit back on his boots. Anything else was out of the question. Edith's knees were sending out painful stabs of protestation. Thelma was quite pleased to be able to achieve the position, and felt wonderfully superior to that awful builder, the woman on the other side of him who was having trouble, and the old woman at the back who had given up. Neville's thoughts had turned to Roz's tight little shorts as his forehead had hit the mat. Malcolm shot Julian an evil look.

"Just time for a quick sip of water and then we'll do some core strengthening. Water machine is in the corner." Petra paused the CD and the room was quiet.

CHAPTER 9

"HAVE YOU DONE something like this before?" Neville didn't quite know what to say to Roz whilst standing in the queue for water, but he wasn't about to let the opportunity slip by.

"No. I've done aerobics mainly, and cycling and jogging. This one's new. My boyfriend is home early on Mondays to look after our son, so this is a little bit of me-time."

Shit! How he hated the word boyfriend…. Neville crept further back in the queue.

"Have you done something like this before?" Neville smiled at a thin-faced woman who looked as if she'd swallowed a wasp.

"No. It's supposed to be good for my back, so I thought I'd give it a go."

"Me too. I've heard it tones the muscles. I'm Neville by the way."

"We'll see. I'm Thelma." Thelma sipped some water and moved back onto her mat.

Well, at least I got a few words out of her! Neville smiled in Thelma's direction and sat down on his mat.

"Hello Mrs Lambert, fancy seeing you here!" Julian poured some water for the old lady and patted her hair.

"Call me Edie, dear. Thank you Julian." Edith took the water, pleased to be recognised.

"Now it's time to do some core strengthening. When the abdominal muscles are toned and strong, then they will protect the lower back area. First off, let's have you all lying in a straight line on your mats, arms by your sides; both sides of the body perfectly in balance." Petra turned the CD back on and there was the sound of waves crashing onto the shore.

Yep, I can do this one, no problem. Thank Christ the whales have stopped mating. Roger lay down on his mat and closed his eyes.

"Now big breath in, exhale and lift those legs up in the air, keeping the feet together."

Up went the legs of Petra and Roz almost in unison, followed by Julian and Malcolm. Neville looked surreptitiously to his right to take a quick look at the wasp woman, whose long slim legs in her Lycra shorts he was beginning to find rather attractive. Judy bit her lip as a large rumbling snore emanated from the prostrate form on her right. In her peripheral vision she could determine that neither Roger nor the old lady seemed to be moving much at all.

"Keep those legs up in the air for another count of 20, and then very slowly lower them down, keeping the feet together and the legs out straight." Petra, lying on the mat with her legs up in the air, thought she could hear somebody snoring.

"Now cross the feet at the ankles and bring the knees up to the chest. Put your hands behind your head. Big breath in, exhale and lift the head and shoulders, keeping the head down towards the chest. Put your right elbow to left knee, and then left elbow to right knee. Keep going with the stomach crunches. Breathe through it; opposite elbow to knee."

God, was she out of condition! Judy couldn't keep the urge to giggle in for much longer. She risked a quick look around; Roger and the old woman were totally out of it, mouths open and breathing deeply, and the old woman's top set of teeth had fallen out. No!... Please! Judy's head dropped back to the mat as waves of uncontrollable laughter washed over her. She'd never laughed so much since Brian's old girlfriend had dressed him up as a woman for a fancy dress party, complete with afro wig, balloon breasts, one of her old dresses and a pair of hold-up stockings.

"Wha-a-at's goin' on?" Judy's laughter had woken Roger, who sat up momentarily dazed to find everybody's legs in the air, all except Judy who had given up and was hugging her knees with tears streaming down her face, and the old woman whose snores he could hear behind him.

"Exhale and bring the head and shoulders down and put the feet to the floor. Arms by your sides please. Glad you're back with us, Roger." Petra sighed and looked up towards the ceiling. Why her? Why did she get always get stuck with these no-hopers?

CHAPTER 10

JUDY TURNED THE key in the lock. She hadn't expected to have had such a laugh. Roger had apologised for falling asleep; they had gently woken up the old lady, and had all agreed to meet up again the following Monday.

"Mum. Elliott's been sick all over the bathroom. It's all brown and disgusting." Marlon walked out of the door just as Judy was walking in.

"Oh God, no. Where are you going?"

"Out."

"Who with?"

"My mates. Be back soon." Marlon sauntered out of the gate in the direction of the park.

Judy sighed and found her youngest son lying on his bed looking a pale shade of green:

"What's the matter? What have you eaten?"

"More like how much has he eaten? There were at least 6 big bars of chocolate to start with judging by the wrappers in the kitchen bin.

"I didn't think you bought chocolate anymore?" Nick, smelling sweetly of aftershave, wafted past Judy on his way to the front door.

"Where are you off to?"

"Out."

"With Tracey?"

"Yeah."

"Nick, I need to speak to you about Tracey."

"If it's the contraceptive lecture, then we've all had that one. Tracey's on the pill."

"Oh. Where's Brian?"

"Out."

"Elliott. How are you?"

"Feeling a bit better now. Sorry, Mum."

"Where did you get all the chocolate from?" "A mate. He gave it to me."

"I need to talk to you about your food intake, Elliott."

"Not now, Mum. I want to go to sleep."

"Tomorrow then."

"Yeah."

Judy sighed and went to find the mop and bucket.

Roger let himself into his flat. He felt wide awake and raring to go after his little doze. He wished he had asked for that Judy bird's number; she was ok, that one. Not as fit as that Roz woman down at the front, but likeable nonetheless. She had been good with the old lady; waking her up and fussing over her. She was obviously used to looking after people. The one that looked like she was sitting on a bee's nest he'd seen somewhere before, but couldn't for the life of him remember where.

Neville sauntered home ruminating on whether to return the following week. There didn't seem much point if none of the women were interested in him: Thelma seemed a bit of a cold fish; Judy looked a bit older, and Roz obviously had a boyfriend. Probably the only one there who would enjoy his company was the old woman. However, by the time he had arrived home he had come to the decision to give it one more week.

Julian had been aware of the strained atmosphere all the

way home in the car, but decided to rise above it. He thought Mal's purple spikes looked the dog's bollocks, so why was he so angry?

"Cut it all off, Julian. Get the clippers and do it now." Malcolm stood looking at himself in the bathroom mirror. "I look like Johnny Rotten gone wrong."

"Sorry, Mal. You look really cool as far as I'm concerned."

"If you don't do it, then I'm going to."

With a heavy sigh Julian set the clippers to number 4, and turned them on. He felt like crying as Malcolm's purple tresses fell all around his feet.

"There. All done. Happy now?"

"Yes. Now piss off and leave me alone."

Thelma could hear the TV blaring out into the street as she opened the garden gate. Her mother was as deaf as a post, but Thelma knew she would rather cut off her arm than admit it. The neighbours would surely be complaining soon:

"It's me, Mum!"

"What?"

"It's only me. I'm back."

"How was the class?" Sylvia wondered whether there was something wrong with the volume on the TV remote control. She couldn't seem to turn it up louder any more.

"Ok. I'm going back next week."

"What'd you say?"

"Nothing. I'm going for a bath."

Edith yawned and opened her front door. She was so embarrassed; fancy falling asleep on the mat! Her teeth had fallen out as well, but Judy had been so kind and told her that it didn't really matter. She must make sure she didn't eat a huge meal next Monday before class; that steak and kidney pudding had really knocked her out.

Roz walked into the kitchen and smelt the aroma of freshly cooked chips. She could hear Mark upstairs putting Jimmy to bed. She wrinkled her nose: the whole house reeked. Heads were going to roll …

CHAPTER 11

THERE WAS ONE mat remaining right at the back when Roz arrived early for the second lesson. Good! That awful Roger wouldn't be able to look at her arse. She had left a delicious nut roast in the oven for Mark and Jimmy, with instructions for them to leave some out for her on a covered plate.

Judy acknowledged Roz as she sat down on the mat next to her. She hoped she wouldn't feel the urge to giggle again, but that builder fellah had made her laugh even if he didn't realise he was doing it.

"Evening. Had a good week?"

"Not too bad. I've been trying new healthy recipes out on my son and boyfriend. The trouble is, I think they'd rather eat fish and chips."

"Tell me about it. I've had to put my youngest son on a diet, but we've all had to eat the same food as I can't bring myself to tell him he's overweight."

"How's he liking the diet?"

"He's not. I've a sneaky feeling he's spending all his pocket money on chocolate and sweets."

Roz smiled sympathetically: "Join the club. My boyfriend's probably cooking chips now to go with the nut roast."

Roger felt clean and fresh in his new tracksuit. His feet were washed and powdered, and he felt ready to take on the world. As he entered the Pilates room he could see Judy at the back talking to the arse on legs. Shit! He was late and would have to sit right at the front with the wooftahs, as the old lady, the wasp woman and the merchant banker were all in the middle row. He vowed to get there early next week, wait outside, and then follow Judy in. He sat down and tried to move his mat away slightly from the poof with the ponytail nearest to him, who was smiling and whispering something to his bald boyfriend in a low voice.

Neville was pleased. He had managed to get a mat next to Thelma, and she had smiled at him as he had seated himself down. What next? What could he say to her? He cleared his throat.

"Haven't I seen you somewhere else before?" Yes, I know it's corny, but it's all I can think of.

"Well, I work in the library in town. You would have probably seen me if you're a regular library user."

"Ah! I knew I'd seen you somewhere before!" Edith suddenly wondered if Thelma was able to recall which books she'd taken out. Neville hid his annoyance at the interruption:

"Yes, that's where I've seen you." Neville had never been to the library before in his life, but made a conscious decision to join in the coming week.

"He just moved his mat away and gave me a dirty look." Julian smiled at Malcolm and kept his voice low. He was so glad they were on speaking terms again.

"So what? Who needs scum like that? Ignore him and perhaps he'll go away."

"Good evening everybody! Have you all had a good week?" Petra tried to sound jollier than she felt. She had menstrual cramps, a headache, and felt like killing somebody. She turned the CD player on and inserted a disc; the sound of what Edith supposed were African children's voices singing in unison filled the room.

"Yes thank you, Petra." Edith thought she'd better speak for the majority, as nobody else had decided to answer.

"Tonight we're going to repeat the stretches we learned last week and learn some more, and then add in some other exercises to strengthen the core musculature. So….let's have everybody standing up on their mats."

Roger felt able to move a little better in a tracksuit and bare feet, and after eating only one small sandwich. He was starving hungry, but decided he would pig out after the class. He could keep up with those poofs and that merchant banker; no trouble! And where did that Petra bird buy her CD's from?

"Feet hip distance apart, stand up tall, press your navel into your back, big breath in, exhale and reach up to the ceiling!" Petra tried to ignore the stab of pain that made her want to double over as she reached up. "Come on… reach up taller than last week!"

Julian had listened to Malcolm's advice, and eager to please him had practiced stretching upwards all week. As he reached up he felt his left arm definitely rise a little higher than it had on the first lesson.

"Hey, this stretching works you know! I'm sure my shoulder feels a bit easier!"

Roger listened with interest. Perhaps the poof would tell him what exercises he'd done? He'd have to try and remember to ask him.

"It will do, Julian. It just takes time and patience." Petra smiled and looked towards the middle of the room. "Exhale as you bring the arms down. Now shake out those shoulders, keep your navel touching your back, and roll down, one vertebra at a time."

Neville could see the back of Roz's head through his shins. Was she at the back on purpose? Had she seen him looking at her arse last week? He took a quick glance to his right and was certain that Thelma had been looking at him for a split second. Did she fancy him?

Edith stayed standing up and felt rather dismayed. Her navel hadn't touched her back since before puberty, and there was no way she could ever bend over like that.

"Walk forward, keeping your heels on the mat. Stretch out those hamstrings! Walk back again, count to thirty, and then roll back up one vertebra at a time, keeping the navel and the pelvic floor pulled in."

Judy was aware through her peripheral vision that the old lady was still standing up. Down at the front she could see that Roger was behaving himself; his feet were bare and he had actually managed to roll down this week, although was having some difficulty in coming back up. Get rid of that beer gut!

"Roll down again and go onto all fours. Make sure both sides are balanced, with knees under hips. Push your navel in, take a deep breath, exhale and raise your back up while pushing your head down, count to thirty and then exhale as you bring the back down and the head up. Repeat this one again folks. It's good for the back."

Thelma felt that maybe Neville was taking secret glances to his right. Did he fancy her? She just had to quickly check that he wasn't looking at her. These men were all the same; sex, sex, sex. It was all they could think about.

Oh God, she'd just caught his eye! Thelma kept her eyes fixed to the front, stayed on all fours, and waited for the next exercise.

"Now we're going to have a bit of fun. Come up to a standing position slowly, and take one of the gym balls at the back of the room. Place it on your mat and sit down on it."

Edith hadn't noticed the gym balls before. She gave them the evil eye as she walked towards them. How was she going to sit down on one of those?

Judy looked to her left. Roz was sitting on the ball as though she sat on one every day of her life.

"It's easy; just copy me!"

Edith looked around as Judy sat on her ball. If she sat on

one of those she'd never be able to get up again….

Roger lifted the ball under his arm. Fucking hell! She's having a tin bath!

"Have you sat on one of these before?" Neville walked back to his mat with Thelma, rolling their balls in front of them.

"No. Let's hope we don't fall off!"

Thelma's face relaxed, and Neville thought there could even have been the hint of a smile. He felt encouraged.

"Don't worry Jules. It's easy when you get your balance." Malcolm decided he wasn't going to laugh at Julian's obvious nervousness as he placed himself gingerly on the ball.

Roger put the ball on his mat and stood looking at it. Shit! The pooftah's sitting on it, so now I've got to give it a go! He lowered himself on to the ball slowly, and gripped the sides for all he was worth.

"Edith, are you going to sit down?" Petra tried to keep her impatience with the old woman under control.

"No, dear. I'll stay standing." Edith felt like crying. She wanted to go home.

CHAPTER 12

"ARE WE ALL sitting comfortably on our balls?"

Roger debated whether or not to come back with the obvious witty retort, and saw that Judy was trying hard not to giggle at the double entendre, but Petra obviously did not think there was much cause for mirth.

"Sit up tall with navels pressed in towards the back and pelvic floor up. Big breath in, exhale, and we'll start by lifting our arms out to the sides."

"Fucking hell! This is terrible!" Roger's ball started to wobble and he forgot to look around for the pelvic floor. The African children's voices reached a crescendo.

"Language, Roger. Keep your navel pulled in and use your legs for balance."

"Sorry."

Judy stifled another giggle. Her thigh muscles were complaining already. How could she have let herself get so out of condition? What was that terrible music?

"Now keep the navel pulled in and the arms outstretched. Lift the right knee up and then stretch that leg out."

Out went Roz's leg straight in front. Neville glanced to his left; Thelma seemed to have managed it. He was just about to give it a go, when he was distracted by a loud thump in front of him.

"Shit!" Roger felt like a prize prat.   He picked himself up from the mat and sat back on the ball.

"Ok, Roger?" Petra ignored giggling from the back of the room.

"Yes, forget it. I'm fine." He was going to master this thing if it killed him!

"Good for you. Get back on and have another go." Petra smiled encouragingly at Roger. "Now everybody, put the right leg down, lift up the left knee and stretch the leg out, keeping the navel in. Don't forget that pelvic floor."

She could see that everybody seemed to have managed it this time, all except the old woman of course, who was still standing up on her mat and looking as though she wanted to be somewhere else.

"Count to thirty, and then bring the leg down. We'll have a little break for a sip of water, and then do another few exercises on the ball afterwards." Petra paused the CD; she'd had enough of that one. She searched in her bag for a replacement.

Roger rubbed his aching left buttock as he stood in the queue for water.

"Did you hurt yourself? Sorry I laughed. I couldn't help it. I just laugh at everything." Judy felt embarrassed and felt she ought to apologise.

"That's ok. I felt a right idiot though."

"You managed to do it afterwards, so good for you." Judy sipped her water as she smiled at Roger. He was overweight, but not bad looking. He still had a mop of thick grey hair and what looked like all his own teeth.

Roger grinned. She was all right, this Judy bird. He'd sure like to have a go at lying down on the mat with her!

"Can I ask you a question?"

"Sure."

"I can't find a pelvic floor. Where is it? That Petra bird keeps going on about it."

Judy felt herself blushing as she giggled again.

"It's the muscles you use to stop yourself weeing."

"Cheers for that darling." Roger wished he hadn't asked, but gave them a little squeeze anyway as he stood in the queue.

"Edie, shall we help you to try and sit on the ball before the class starts again?" Julian and Malcolm stood either side of Edith. They both felt sorry for the old lady.

"You can try dears, but I won't be able to get up though."

"I'll take one arm and Malcolm will hold your other arm. There! What do you think?"

Edith sat carefully on the ball. It took all her powers of balance and concentration to keep upright. Her thigh muscles felt like jelly after even a few minutes.

"Help me up, boys. It's terrible. I'm going to go arse over tit in a minute."

Judy giggled at the mental image of Edith falling backwards over the ball, legs akimbo. Why did she find everything so hysterical? She glanced across at Thelma, who always looked as if her face had never cracked a smile in its life.

Wait: Yes; actually it was smiling! The business-type had obviously said something to pull its chain......

"For the rest of the lesson we will be doing some more gym ball work. Are we all sitting on our balls? Edith, what about you?" Petra thought she already knew the answer to that one.

"No dear, I'll just sit here and watch." Edith lowered herself down stiffly onto the mat.

"Whatever you want. Everybody else sit as tall as you can, with navels pulled into the back. Now roll down on the ball, one vertebra at a time, and touch the floor with your outstretched hands." Petra put a CD into the player.

Tricky. Tricky. Roger hoped the ball didn't slide out from under him, bash him onto his arse, and set Judy off giggling again. He sighed at the sound of the whales mating again. Why couldn't they just do the exercises in silence?

Neville, head upside down, risked the quickest of glances to his right and was just in time to catch Thelma's head as it turned away from him with lightning speed. Should he suggest a drink in the bar downstairs after the class? What if she said no?

"Now roll up slowly, then walk the ball forward, place your legs a bit wider apart for balance, and drape yourselves backwards over it. See if you can touch the floor with your fingers. This is very good for stretching out the lower back."

Roz was draped in a second, fingers touching the floor, but immediately realising a new problem: Now they'll both have full view of her open legs!

Neville had an interesting view of Roz's tiny shorts as he bent himself backwards over the ball. Roger tried hard to focus upside down on Roz's open legs two rows directly behind him without the merchant banker getting in the way. As he rolled the ball a bit to the left to get a better look, there was an ominous wobble.

"Shit!" Roger could hear Judy's stifled laughter as he picked himself up. He'd fallen onto the same bruised buttock as before.

"All right, Roger?" Petra pulled herself up from the ball to check on her pupil.

"No problem. Everything's peachy." Bastard ball!

"We'll finish the class with a few more stretches. Edith, you'll be able to do this one. Roll the balls to the back, and then lie on your front on your mats."

"I can't lie on my front, dear. My bust is too big."

"Just lay on your back then and stretch out."

Judy had a vision of two enormous wobbling breasts standing up alone on an exercise mat. She rammed her head down between her arms and into the foam mat, and tried to stop her shoulders from shaking.

"Grab your toes, big breath in, exhale and lift yourselves up!" Petra looked at the clock and saw to her relief that there was only another five minutes to go.

"Breathe through it, count to thirty, and slowly lower yourselves down. Then stretch out on your front with arms in front of you." Petra hoped the old lady hadn't drifted off to sleep again, as her eyes were closed. "Big breath in; exhale, and then lift your arms and legs to form a curve. Keep breathing through it. Very good Roz!"

Using her peripheral vision Judy could see that Roz had formed a perfect arc. Everybody else had slumped back down on their mats, including herself.

"Last stretch for the lower back. Sit back on your heels, then bend forward with arms outstretched and touch the mat with your forehead. Count to thirty." Petra gave a sigh of relief: "Well done! That's all for this week. Give yourselves a clap!" She turned off the CD and gathered her things together.

As Neville retrieved his fleecy jacket from the side table, he reasoned it was going to be now or never:

"It's thirsty work this Pilates isn't it!"

"Yes." Thelma collected her bag and wondered what was coming next.

"Fancy a quick orange juice in the bar downstairs?" He held his breath.

"Mother will be waiting for me at home."

"Ten minutes won't make much of a difference."

"Oh. All right then, but just the once."

Neville's sigh of relief was audible even to Judy, as she grabbed her handbag. Perhaps she'll have cracked a smile by next week? As she made her way out of the room, she bumped into Roger who seemed to be hanging about outside.

"Sorry again for laughing, Roger. Really, I should know better at my age."

"No worries. Do you live nearby?"

"Yes, on the Kingsland estate. I've got to run and get the bus now before I miss it. See you next week!"

Roger thought it was now or never. Seize the day!

"Can I give you a lift home? It's not good for women to hang around bus stops late at night."

"I don't want to put you to any trouble."

"No trouble at all. I've got to go that way."

"Oh, all right then. Thanks very much."

Judy thought that maybe there might be a gentleman trying to get out from beneath Roger's chauvinistic exterior.

CHAPTER 13

"YOU CAN HAVE something stronger if you like?" Neville thought that maybe several double brandies might do the trick.

"An orange juice is fine. Thank you."

A man had never before asked Thelma out for a drink. Her mother had always told her they were only after one thing, and to keep her hand on her halfpenny. Well, one orange juice at the leisure centre wouldn't hurt!

"Do you just live with your mother then?"

Neville looked approvingly at Thelma's shoulder length wavy auburn hair and suddenly had a mental picture of her turning into a harridan wearing curlers and a headscarf.

"Yes. Dad died two years ago now, but Mum's finding it difficult to cope."

"I only left home five years ago. I had a similar problem actually. My sisters were married, and I was the only one left after Dad died. He was quite young when he went unfortunately. Mum started to cling, so I moved out for her sake and for mine. She's joined several clubs since I've gone, and I even think she's now got a boyfriend on the sly, so it did us both a world of good in the long run."

Thelma nodded as she sipped her drink. Here was somebody who understood her problem! She gave a rueful laugh.

"Perhaps I should try that. It'll probably cause World War

Three though. She'll be phoning around the family telling them how terrible I am for leaving her all alone."

"You're entitled to a life of your own. She's had one, and so should you." Neville never thought it would be so easy to talk to somebody.

"Yes, you're right. I know you're right, but it's just so hard to make the break when you're an only child. I'm all Mum's got now."

"I had that feeling even though I've got sisters. They live up North and can't visit that often. I started to resent Mum for clinging to me the way she did. I was suffocating, unable to even pop out to the pub for half an hour without her caus-.ing a scene."

"Anyway, thanks for the drink." Thelma stood up. "I'd best get back now before Mum sends out the search parties. See you next week at Pilates."

"My pleasure. We can do this again before next Monday if you like." Neville held his breath again:

"What were you thinking of then? Perhaps Saturday evening?" Thelma hoped she didn't sound too forward.

"Saturday's fine. Eight o'clock? I'd give you a lift back now, but my car's at home. I only live around the corner."

"No, I've got my car. See you here at the bar then on Saturday."

She had a date! Thelma virtually skipped all the way back to her car.

"Just pull up here please, near to that dodgy-looking mob standing over by my front gate."

Judy recognised Elliott standing in the garden with a group of his friends. They looked in her direction as she got out of the car.

"Thanks for the lift, Roger. See you next week."

No wedding ring. Get in there!

"Is your kettle working?"

"Yes, why?"

"I'd love a cup of tea. I'm parched."

"It's a madhouse in there."

"Well that's just fine. I'll fit right in then."

"Elliott, this is Roger, a friend from Pilates."

"How's it going Elliott?"

Roger saw a sullen-looking overweight teenager giving him the once over as he walked through the garden gate.

"Ok." Elliott looked past Roger. "Mum, can I have an advance on my pocket money?"

"No. We've already discussed this." Judy sighed and opened the front door. "Marlon! Turn the music down please!" She turned to Roger; "See, I told you it was a madhouse."

"How many children have you got then?"

"Four teenage boys. It sounds like they're all in tonight as well."

Shit!

"A houseful of men, what with your husband and all."

"Even the cat was male until he had a little trip to see the vet. No husband; I'm divorced."

"Who's this?" Brian stood in the kitchen doorway with arms folded. Judy smiled and likened him to a tomcat protecting its territory.

"Brian, this is Roger, a friend from Pilates."

"How's it going, Brian?" Roger stood up and shook hands. Good God, he's built like a brick shit house!

"Good thanks. I'm off down the gym now. Nick's in the front room with Tracey. Probably best to leave them to it."

"Have you got any children?" Judy placed two cups of tea on

the kitchen table and looked at Roger with interest.

"One son, Lewis. He lives with his mother and the wonderful Barry. I see him during the week at work though. I got him a job with me; he's learning the building trade."

"My ex-husband Alan washed his hands of our boys. I make sure he pays his whack though. I work in the local GP surgery on the reception desk. We get by, just."

"I'm off round Tracey's." Nick popped his head around the kitchen door.

"Roger, this is my second eldest, Nick."

"How's it going, Nick? I'm a friend of your Mum's from Pilates." Roger stood up again and extended his hand to another well-muscled young man.

"Ok, ta."

"Have you got your key? I'll probably be in bed when you get home."

"Yeah. See you later."

"Anyway; I need to sort out my youngest two now, and make sure they've done their homework." Judy stood up. "Thanks for the lift."

"No problem. Cheers for the tea." Roger decided to throw caution to the wind; "If you fancy going to the pub for a drink on Saturday night I can pick you up about 7.30 if you like?"

Judy was taken by surprise. No man had shown any interest in her at all since the divorce. She'd better seize the day and make the most of it.

"That sounds very nice, thanks."

Roger smiled as he started up the car.

Yes!

CHAPTER 14

"SLOW DOWN, JIMMY, wait for me!"

As Roz jogged past the usual gaggle of gossiping women walking along the footpath to the village school she was rapidly coming to the conclusion that you could lead a man to healthy food, but you couldn't make him eat it. When she'd returned home the previous night from Pilates, the smell of frying bacon had still been in the air. The delicious nut roast had been taken out of the oven, two tiny slices had been cut from it, but the rest had been left for her. It was clear that Mark and Jimmy had visited the late night supermarket as soon as her back was turned.

After making sure Jimmy's bike was secure, she kissed her son and watched him run into his classroom. Wasn't she doing the right thing in giving him healthy food in his lunchbox? Should she give him cake, crisps, jam sandwiches and sweets then, like all the other children? Surely that was child cruelty? Surely it was up to her to safeguard her son's arteries while he was still too young to realise the dangers in eating saturated fat?

Roz started the jog back home, keeping her gaze down on the ground as she passed by the mothers straggling in through the school gates. Why was life so difficult? Why didn't they like her?

By the time she had reached the front door, Roz had decided to add one small bag of low fat crisps to Jimmy's hummus and salad wraps and fat free yoghurt the next day. Perhaps that would make his lunchbox more acceptable amongst his classmates, and less open to ridicule.

Julian's heart sank as the familiar figure of Edie walked through the door of the salon:

"Hello Edie! What's it to be today then?" *Whatever it is, it'll turn out to be another cauliflower....*

"Morning Julian. I fancy a bit of colour today; something different; a new me!

"Now you're talking! Shall we go ash blonde? Here's the sample." He held up a colour chart in front of the old lady.

"Yes. Ash blonde it is then, dear."

"They won't recognise you at Pilates next Monday."

"I've had enough of Pilates. It's too hard for me at my age. I should have done it years ago. Too late now, because the old bones won't bend."

"Sorry to hear that. We'll still see you at the salon though?"

"Oh yes. I'll be along again in a fortnight. You never know dear, I might have the courage then to even ask you to do a different style."

"I'll look forward to it, Edie."

"How's that? I've taken a bit off the top as well."

"I like it, dear. Just so long as I don't look like I've got a cauliflower for a head."

Julian bit his lip.

CHAPTER 15

"YOU'RE NOT GOING out again are you?"

Her mother's voice had that familiar whine to it as she watched her daughter combing her hair in the mirror.

"Yes, I'm meeting a man in a bar." Thelma smoothed down her black cocktail dress and thought she'd get the argument over with straight away.

"What?"

"I said do you know where I left the keys to the car?" She suddenly decided she couldn't face another scene while feeling so excited.

"No, I haven't seen them." Sylvia's face took on a sulky look, but Thelma decided to rise above it.

"I won't be late back. I'm meeting a friend for a drink."

"Who is she?"

"Somebody from the Pilates class."

"Can I come? I'll pay for the drinks. It'll be my treat."

"Not tonight, Mum. Another time." No! No! No!

"Well, I'll wait up for you."

Thelma sighed as she opened the front door. When would she ever be free? She was 33 years old for God's sake!

Perched on a bar stool at the leisure centre, Neville once

again watched everybody who came in through the door. His heart was racing with excitement, as this time he actually knew what his date was going to look like. Any moment now a tall, slim woman with auburn hair would open the door. How was he going to keep the conversation going all night?

Thelma turned off the car's engine and checked her hair in the rear view mirror. She'd been wary of men all her life, but this one seemed very nice. He'd been into the library a couple of times that week as well; she was sure she hadn't seen him in there before.

Taking a deep breath, she opened the door to the bar. She saw him straight away, sitting on one of the bar stools. He waved to her and she smiled as she walked towards him, approving of his rather expensive-looking grey three-piece pin-stripe suit and tie.

"Where's your Rolling Stones t-shirt then?"

"Well, I thought I'd push the boat out tonight, so to speak." Neville was amazed at how much more attractive Thelma was when she smiled. She didn't look half bad either in that little black number. "Can I get you a drink?"

"Orange juice please." She had to keep her wits about her, just in case...

Thelma daintily sipped her drink and kept her knees tightly together. Was he looking at her legs? Had her dress ridden up too much as she sat down?

"How's your Mum? Did she mind you going out?" Neville tried to keep his eyes on Thelma's face, but his gaze wanted to travel down to her lovely slim legs encased in black nylons.

"She hates me going anywhere. Everywhere I go she wants to come with me. It's a nightmare."

"I had the same trouble. My old Mum once wanted to come on holiday to Spain with me and a few University mates when we'd all passed our finals."

Thelma laughed at the mental image of an old lady trailing around haughtily after her drunken son and his friends.

"They can't let go, can they? They can't see that we have a

life of our own!”

“Mum got the message eventually though. When I was able to buy my own place she suddenly learned to drive, joined over 60’s social clubs, and started enjoying herself.”

“Wow! I can never imagine my mother doing any of that. Perhaps she should meet up with yours and learn a few lessons.”

“That can be arranged I’m sure.”

Thelma pulled her dress down as much as she could.

“You’re a quick reader. You were back in the library in record time.”

“I realised when I got home that I’d read them all before.” Neville hoped she would fall for the little white lie.

“I’ve read most of the books in that library over the years. Mum always complains that I’ve got my nose in a book. Actually, it’s the only way I can shut myself off and escape.”

Thelma wondered if the last remark had given too much away. She must be careful and keep her guard up.

“Would you like to go somewhere else this evening, perhaps to the cinema? There’s a good film on I think.”

“I told Mum I wouldn’t be late. I think we’d better stay here.” Who knows what might happen in the dark in the cinema?

“Ok. Perhaps we could go to the cinema next Saturday night then?” Neville held his breath as he looked at Thelma.

“That would be very nice. I’ll get a local paper and see what’s on.”

Thelma could hear what sounded like a sigh of relief. She wondered what else they could talk about.

“Where do you work, Neville?”

“I work from home. I’m an accountant and also offer financial advice. I have a little downstairs study that I use as an office.”

"You probably don't get to see many people then during the week?" Thelma kicked herself and hoped Neville hadn't assumed by her comment that she thought he was a sad-bag.

"On the contrary. I'm out visiting clients every day. It's great working for myself. If I want to take a long lunch, change my library books and chat to the library staff I don't have to worry about getting back to work by a certain time. Neville smiled as he drank his beer. He was actually getting somewhere with this one…

"Fancy some dinner?"

Thelma could hear her mother's voice inside her head.

'Have lunch with a man but never dinner, because after the main course he'll only have one thing on his mind….'

"I ate earlier, but I could still eat something small."

"Done. There's a nice restaurant in the High Street next to the church. We could get a salad or something."

"Ok."

Thelma stood up and smoothed down her dress. She felt suddenly full of trepidation at the thought of what was going to happen at the end of the evening, but now the night was young and it was time to break free of her mother's shackles.

CHAPTER 16

"CAN YOU MAKE it a tenner instead, Mum? I've got to babysit two of them."

Brian pushed his luck and wondered whether his mother would give in. She seemed to be in a good mood lately.

"Haven't you just been paid?"

Judy fished in her purse for a ten-pound note. There was only one left, and she handed it over reluctantly to her eldest son.

"Great. Thanks Mum." Brian took the note quickly before his mother changed her mind. "I'm still only an apprentice. The money's nearly gone now."

"Welcome to my world." Judy hoped that Roger wouldn't want her to pay for a round of drinks later at the pub.

"What time is he coming round then?"

Brian wasn't sure he liked the thought of a total stranger trying to get into his mother's knickers, but the babysitting money would sure come in handy.

"Half past seven."

"Phone me if you have any problems."

Judy hid a smile.

Roger cleaned his razor and patted on some aftershave.   As he replaced the bottle top he read the label once more; 212 Sexy Men. Perhaps Judy might think he was a candidate for number 213? He looked at his paunch in the mirror and sucked in his stomach, letting it out again with a sigh. Hmmm… perhaps not; might still need to do a bit more of that Pilates malarkey….

Driving down the maze of alleys on the Kingsland estate he recognised Judy's house by the usual gang of teenagers hanging around in the front garden. The youngest son stood in the open doorway talking to his friends; his oversized body almost touching either side of the doorframe.

"Evening, Elliott. How's it going? Is your Mum there?" Roger walked up to the front door and ignored the fact that the boy was blocking his entry.

"Dunno. Haven't seen her."

Roger pressed the doorbell and looked over the boy's shoulder into the hallway. He could see the brick shit-house approaching.

"Evening Brian. How's it going? Is your Mum there?" He wanted to punch the fat kid's lights out, but realised this act of aggression wouldn't sit well with the hunk of muscle standing in front of him.

"She's getting ready. Elliott, move out of the way, you wanker. Come in Roger."

"Cheers."

Loud rapping music could be heard coming from one of the bedrooms. Did that one ever come out of his bedroom? Roger sat down on the well-worn sofa and looked around the lounge. The walls were full of photos of the boys at various ages, but there were none featuring Judy's ex-husband. Roger wondered how he might measure up to the absent Alan.

"Where are you off to tonight then?"

Brian remained standing and looked down at Roger while flexing his biceps. Roger tried to ignore the overt display of masculine muscle power: Shit; he'd once looked like that before middle-age had caught up with him. Now he was just pleased not to have that bloody pain in his shoulder all the time.

"Just down to the local pub I expect. Not far."

"I'm going clubbing at 11."

"So, I'll have your Mum back at quarter to then."

The testosterone-filled youth was starting to get on Roger's nerves already. With some relief he heard Judy's light footsteps on the stairs.

"Sorry Roger, I'm running a bit late. I had to go down to the park and find Elliott. Brian's looking after him tonight."

"Only until 10:45, then I'm going clubbing with Shaz." Brian turned his gaze away from Roger and onto his mother.

"We'll be back before then. Tell Marlon to turn the music down after ten."

Roger looked appreciably at Judy as she entered the room in a waft of perfume; an oasis of femininity prettying up the mostly male domain. He wanted to pick her up in his arms and take her away from it all.

"See you later." Roger stood up and was pleased to find he was more or less the same height as Brian.

"Yeah."

Roger virtually pushed past Elliott, still standing in the doorway, in his efforts to get Judy out of the house. There was no way he'd ever be able to get to know her better at home with all four boys always hanging about.

"Where would you like to go then?"

He couldn't take his eyes off her. She was wearing a pretty frilly sort of top that came down low on her chest, and tight jeans that showed off her womanly figure.

"We'd best just go to the pub on the estate. It's only around the corner. Come on, I'll show you."

Judy was aware that Roger's eyes were out on stalks. She felt good about herself, and pleased that the man walking along by her side was definitely finding her attractive.

Judy nodded to a few people she knew as they entered the pub, and Roger steered her over to an empty table near the bar:

"What can I get you?"

"Gin and tonic please." Thank goodness she didn't have to pay.

"Cheers Roger, thanks for the drink."

"My pleasure. Isn't that one of your sons that's just come in?" Bastard. The brick shit-house probably told him to keep an eye out.

Judy turned towards the door and giggled.

"Oh yes, that's Nick with Tracey." She smiled at them as they came over.

"Hey Roger. Nice to meet you again." Roger found his hand being held in a vice-like grip.

"How's it going Nick? Alright Tracey?" Surely they weren't going to sit with them all night?

"Great thanks. Nick, can we have game of snooker in a minute? The table's empty." Tracey put her arms around Nick's waist and placed her head on his shoulder.

Yes, do. Fuck off…..

"Ok. Just going to get a pint first."

Judy laughed as they walked towards the bar:

"That'll be a pint of orange juice. The barman knows he's underage. Every time he comes in here he tries his luck, but Mike knows he's not 18 until November."

"The only thing I can recall about being 18 is getting absolutely bladdered on my birthday, and waking up feeling like death the next morning." Roger drank half of his pint of beer in one go, wanting to be out and away from the sight of yet another of Judy's sons as quickly as possible. "Do you want to go on somewhere else?"

"No, this is fine. I'm happy sitting here and chatting, if that's ok with you?" Judy smiled and sipped her gin and tonic.

"Yeah, fine."
Shit.

"Yeah, fine."
Shit.

CHAPTER 17

"THAT WAS A lovely dinner. Thanks Neville. I didn't think I could eat all that, but it was too nice to leave. I think I'd better be getting back now though."

Thelma hadn't enjoyed herself so much in ages. It had been easier finding something to talk about all evening than she'd first thought.

"My pleasure. I'll walk you back to your car."

Neville wondered whether to risk slipping his hand in hers as they walked back along the High Street. However, he thought better of it and instead concentrated on walking on the outside of the pavement nearer the road, just as his mother had taught him.

"Don't forget our cinema date next Saturday, and I'll see you at Pilates on Monday." He wondered whether to give Thelma a kiss before she got into her car, but changed his mind at the last minute.

"I'll look forward to it. Bye, Neville." Thelma closed the car door and turned the engine on, slightly disappointed that Neville hadn't even tried to give her a kiss at all.

At half past ten as Roger walked Judy back home he was conscious of the fact that Nick and Tracey had also exited the pub and were following a discreet distance behind.

"Fancy doing this again next weekend? There's a nice pub near where I live. There's usually a band playing there on Saturdays as well." And none of your boys know where it is…..

"If you like, yeah it sounds great." Judy was beginning to like this rough-and-ready builder a bit more; "What sort of music?"

"Rock covers mostly." Roger could see the brick shit-house standing in the doorway. He knew there was no way he was going to be allowed to get past him for a coffee unless he thumped him one. The other brick shit-house walking behind was stepping up the pace.

"I'll see you on Monday at Pilates, and then we can arrange times. I'll pick you up in the car; it'll save you waiting around for the bus." He thought it best to admit defeat and try again the following week.

"Fine. Thanks for a nice evening Roger."

"See you Monday."

He felt like a teenager, standing at the garden gate with the girl's parents at the front door, except now it was all arse-about-tit. The other Neanderthal was almost breathing down his neck as well.

"All right Mum?" Brian opened the gate for his mother and stood in front of Roger in the garden with his arms folded.

"Of course. Why wouldn't I be?"

"Just asking. Elliott and Marlon have gone to bed. Have you got a tenner?"

"No, you took my last one."

"Oh yeah."

Judy turned and waved goodbye to Roger. Under that bluff exterior she thought there was definitely a gentleman trying his best to get out. She began to look forward to the following Saturday, and began to hum to herself as she climbed the stairs to her bedroom.

Opening the door of Marlon and Elliot's room to check on them she could see Elliott was indeed asleep, but that the other bed was empty. Instead, she could see Marlon with his back to her and hunched over their computer with headphones on, completely oblivious to all that was going on around him. On the screen she could see an older man and a young, attractive blonde lady in the act of cunnilingus, and she suddenly realised why Marlon was spending so much time upstairs, supposedly doing his 'school work' on the computer. Shocked, she walked over to the desk and stood in front of her son's line of vision.

"What's going on here?" She whispered as loudly as she could, so as not to wake up Elliott. Marlon was horrified, jumped up and quickly shut the screen down to black.

"Sorry Mum. It was one of Brian's sites. I saw it while I was researching a history project."

"Turn it off and go to bed. We'll discuss this in the morning. I'm very disappointed in you, Marlon."

"Brian and Nick look at it. Why can't I?"

"Brian is nearly five years' older than you, and Nick is almost 18. They are adults and you are not."

"My mates watch it."

"Then your mates' parents are obviously not looking after their children's welfare."

Judy sighed as she walked back to her bedroom. The boys needed a father to explain the male perspective on sex and relationships. She didn't want Marlon (or indeed any of the other boys) growing up viewing females as sex objects for male gratification. A thought suddenly hit her as she climbed into bed: Oh shit; she would have to do the explaining. She was now their father as well as their mother. Their father had had a mid-life crisis and gone off with somebody 15 years' younger than him who looked not unlike the girl receiving oral sex that she'd just seen on the screen.

CHAPTER 18

PETRA TURNED ON the CD player and noticed that Neville and Thelma were sitting quite close together on their mats and chatting quite animatedly, waiting for the latecomers to arrive. There was no sign of the old lady. Roger and Judy arrived in a flurry together five minutes after the class should have begun.

"Sorry Petra, I was learning how to do something on the computer and forgot the time."

After checking with a colleague in the know at work earlier that day, Judy was certain that Marlon would have no idea how to turn off the parental lock. No more covert sex lessons for him.

"That's ok. Tonight it's all about concentrating on your breathing. I know you can all breathe without even thinking about it, but with Pilates you have to learn to breathe correctly for the muscles to receive the increased oxygen they need to perform the exercises. It's good to learn to breathe in slowly through the nose for a count of eight, and then out slowly through the mouth for a count of eight." She looked around; they all seemed to be sitting up and taking notice. "Let's do our stretching exercises first and warm up. Stand up tall with navel pulled in and pelvic floor up; big breath in, and let's raise those arms in the air. Exhale as you bring them down again."

Julian listened attentively to what he recognised were Gregorian chants emanating from the CD player, and was pleased that his shoulder didn't seem as painful now as it had been. He'd been stretching upwards every day, and tonight he could raise both his arms to almost the same height. He'd started power-walking on the treadmill at Malcolm's gym after work, and was beginning to feel a lot better in himself. Malcolm's hair was growing back, and when Julian had tentatively asked him if he'd ever considered going blonde, to his surprise he had seemed quite keen on the idea. However, listening to the chanting and thinking about Malcolm going blonde made him forget to concentrate on breathing correctly, and irritatingly he found he was breathing in when he should have been breathing out.

Roz exhaled as she brought her arms down. She'd got this technique sorted already. What she needed to get sorted was her relationship with Mark. Was she prepared to surrender control of what he ate just to please him, even though she knew what he wanted to eat would eventually kill him? How could she stand by and watch him slowly commit suicide? And what was that God-awful music? She followed Petra and lifted her arms in the air again, but the irritating droning and thoughts of Mark committing suicide by eating thousands of bacon rolls made her forget to breathe in at the same time. With a *tut* of annoyance she tried to focus her mind on the job in hand.

"Shake those shoulders out and then roll down slowly, one vertebra at a time." From her vantage point in front of the class, Petra could see Neville and Thelma, arses in the air, turning to smile at each other whilst touching their toes. Roger and Judy, similarly placed, were grinning at each other like Cheshire cats. Something was going on here......

"Now come up slowly with navel and pelvic floor pulled in, and let's stretch out those shoulders. Bring your right arm right around to your left shoulder and support the right elbow with your left hand as you turn your head to the left. Then do the same on the other side."

Roger looked at Judy's profile as she turned her head. She was definitely a little cracker! He'd make sure none of the four Neanderthals would be around on their next date…

"Stand tall with navel in and shoulders back. Big breath in, then exhale and lift the right arm up and over your head. Feel that stretch down the side. Bring the arm down as you breathe in, then exhale and then lift the left arm up and over your head. If you remember to exhale with effort, then the breathing will begin to make sense. Remember the two e's; exhale and effort."

Roger didn't care whether he was breathing in or breathing out. How could he concentrate on doing that, lift his arms up and down while listening to that terrible racket, and think about Judy all at the same time? Fuck that…. Petra wouldn't have a clue whether he was breathing in or out anyway…..

"Now grab your gym balls, sit on them and work your hips around in a circular motion from left to right, and then back the other way. Pretend you've got a hula hoop. Come on; big circles. Let's loosen up that lower back."

Neville smiled at Thelma as they sat side by side on their balls. He wanted to stretch his hand out towards hers, but thought better of it. Thelma smiled back.

"Roll down on your ball and touch left hand to right foot, and then right hand to left foot. Remember those navels everybody."

Roger wondered whether Petra had a navel fetish.

"Now then; here's a challenge for you: Lie down on your mats and put the ball between your feet. Make sure your back is flat to your mat and your navel is pulled in. Put your feet either side of the ball, big breath in through the nose for a count of eight, then exhale through the mouth for a count of eight as you lift that ball up in the air. Pass it to your hands and then over your head to the floor while lowering the legs and keeping the navel pulled in. Big breath in through the nose, then exhale through the mouth, lift the legs and pass the ball back over your head to rest between the feet again.

Lower the legs and repeat." Petra waited for the fun to begin. She didn't have to wait for long. She literally had never seen quite such a balls-up. Balls were going in all directions; Judy's ball at one stage seemed to be covering her face while her shoulders heaved with suppressed mirth. Roger's ball had somehow scooted across the room and crashed into Mal-colm's, knocking it from his hands as he was lowering it to the floor. Neville had given up and was looking to see how Thelma was getting on. He was pleased to see she was look-ing at him to see how he was doing, and they smiled briefly at each other again. The only one seemingly competent was Roz, whose perfect breathing and quiet concentration had ensured the task was being carried out with perfect accuracy.

"This is fucking impossible!" Roger retrieved his ball, went back to his mat, and instead watched appreciatively as Judy lifted her legs in the air.

"Language, Roger." Petra's dislike of the rough builder was increasing with every session.

"Sorry, but I hate these bloody things." Roger kicked his ball to the back of the room and sat down on his mat with a sigh.

"Ok. Let's do some more exercises on your mats. This time we'll have everybody lying on their fronts please."

Roger turned over on his front and found himself with an interesting view of Roz at the back of the room. Stuck up Miss Prim. He wasn't interested any more.......Judy was worth ten of her......if only there weren't so many arseholes of sons!

"We're going to reach behind and grab our toes. Ready? Deep breath in, exhale and lift. The aim of the exercise is to make an arc. Ok?"

"I don't know about making an arc, but it's making me sweat!" Julian wondered if he'd ever been as uncomfortable in his whole life as he was at the present moment.

"That's because you're unfit!" Malcolm hissed in his ear, "You need to come out running with me instead of just power-walking. When you get fitter you'll stop sweating so much."

"Ok. Ok. I'll do it. Just don't keep going on about it!" Malcolm's arc seemed effortless, and Julian felt just a twinge of jealousy.

"You don't have to be so touchy. I'm only suggesting it for your own good."

"Good try everybody. Now stay on your fronts, stretch out on your mats, and think about the next lift. Your arms will stay stretched out at the front, and you'll lift both arms at the same time as lifting both legs. Again, the aim is to make an arc. Ready? Big breath in, navel pulled back, exhale and lift!"

"Christ! My back'll never be the same again!" Roger didn't know how much longer he could stick it for.

"Just another few seconds, Roger. It's good for lower back suppleness."

"Bollocks." Roger had the sense to whisper it under his breath as his muscles screamed for release.

"I heard that." Judy grinned as she looked straight ahead and concentrated on her lift.

"And….relax!" There was an audible sigh as bodies flopped onto mats. Roger hoped the end of the session was in sight. He was sick of feeling a right prat in front of Judy.

CHAPTER 19

THE AROMA OF something that was definitely not the quorn casserole she'd left out hit Roz as soon as she turned the key in the door. She was starving, and the smell soon started to make her mouth water.

"Hi Mummy!" Jimmy came out from his bedroom to greet her at the top of the stairs.

"Shouldn't you be asleep?" Roz smiled and ran up to give her son a kiss.

"We had to wait for the delivery man."

"What delivery man?"

"The one who delivers the pizzas."

"I see. Come on, into bed now. You've got school to-morrow."

Mark looked up from the television screen as she entered the living room.

"Hi. How was your class? Good?"

"Not bad. I can smell something cheesy."

"Yeah. We had pizza for dinner." "What about the quorn casserole?"

"It wasn't doing it for me, or Jimmy for that matter."

"Is it worth me cooking at all then? It seems I'm the only one eating it." She could feel her anger starting to rise.

"Well, it's like this." Mark turned off the TV and turned his attention to Roz. "We're blokes. We like blokes' food. I love you to bits and you've got a great body, but I don't want to eat any more quorn, cous cous, tofu, or hummus; especially no hummus. I want fry ups, curries, bangers and mash, steak pies and chips; all the things that other blokes take for granted."

Roz sighed. She'd lost control.

"But the food you want to eat will kill you in the end!"

"We're all going to die in the end. There's only two things certain in this life; death and taxes. It's just that when I do die I'll be a bit happier if it's bacon butties that have killed me at 75, rather than living to 105 and having to eat nut roasts all that time."

"Can we compromise and have a healthy eating day at least once a week?"

Roz had lost the battle, but maybe there was still a bit of pride that could be salvaged.

"Once a week then, but no hummus. It's like eating feet."

"I'll have to cook two different dinners at night then, because I'm not eating what you and Jimmy eat."

"That's your choice, but it's good that we all still have that choice."

Roz sat herself down on the sofa and put her arms around him.

"Nobody seems to like me." She sighed. "Do you? Do you still love me, Mark?"

"Of course I do. Loads. Get 'em off and I'll show you."

CHAPTER 20

NEVILLE PACED UP and down outside the cinema. Would she show up? It had gone past 7.30 now, and the film would start in 10 minutes.

Suddenly he could hear footsteps running behind him. He did a quick about-turn and there she was, flapping and flustered.

"Sorry I'm late. Mum made a scene and I had to calm her down." Thelma's relief that he was still waiting for her was evident even to Neville.

"That's ok. Let's go in; the film's going to start soon."

Neville actually didn't give two hoots about which film was showing. Instead he had started to think about whether he should tentatively reach out and hold Thelma's hand undercover of the darkness, and his heart had begun to race with anticipation. What sort of reaction would he receive?

They found somewhere to sit near the back. Thelma was nervous as she settled herself down in her seat. Would Neville try anything? No man had ever tried to kiss her before or even ask her out, apart from Neville. She was past 30 and still a virgin. What was going to happen? She knew she was never going to be able to concentrate on watching the film; that was certain.

Neville took a deep breath as the lights went down. It was now or never; he just couldn't wait a moment longer. Surreptitiously looking across to his left to check the location of Thelma's right hand, he wiped his hand on the side of his trousers, mentally crossed his fingers and toes, then reached over and carefully put her hand in his. It felt warm and a little clammy. He waited to be slapped around the face with her other hand, but nothing happened. He breathed an out-ward sigh of relief, as he tried to quieten his pounding heart whilst pretending to be engrossed in watching the screen.

Thelma glanced across at Neville, who seemed absorbed in the trailers. His hand was sweaty, but she was inordinately happy; he liked her and was trying to tell her so in a roundabout way. Both of their hands were damp with nerves, but Thelma wanted the moment to last forever. She looked back at the screen with the ghost of a smile on her lips.

Neville was aware that Thelma was gazing in his direction. By the time he had gathered up enough courage to look at her he found that disappointingly she had turned towards the screen again. However, she hadn't slapped his face at all, and that was good. It was therefore time to plot his next manoeuvre.

An hour into the film and Thelma was starting to get a little uncomfortable. Their entwined hands were slimy with sweat, and she was desperate to go to the Ladies' and plunge both hands under a stream of cold water. Excusing herself she made her way to the lavatory and turned on the cold tap until the water was running at full force. Closing her eyes in blissful relief she lost herself in the moment and let the jet of cool liquid wash over her outstretched palms.

Neville took the chance and wiped the palms of his hands on his seat. He kept his eyes on the entrance and watched for Thelma's return. When he saw her coming towards him he gave them another wipe for good measure. He hoped she didn't ask him what had happened in the story while she'd been gone, as unfortunately he had absolutely no idea at all.

Thelma sat down again and smiled at Neville. He took her hand again, finding it cool and dry. He returned her smile, and decided he hadn't felt as happy as this in a very long time.

He thought the time was right to go one stage further: Removing his hand, he held his breath and let his left arm slide around her shoulders.

Thelma's heart was pounding in her chest. No man had ever wanted to cuddle her before. She became aware of the proximity of his body and felt an unfamiliar stirring sensation in her loins. His right hand reached across to hold her hand again, and she rested her head on his shoulder. She closed her eyes; she didn't want the film to ever end.

Neville hoped his erection wasn't obvious. He shifted uncomfortably in his seat and crossed his legs. His cheeks burned with embarrassment; in fact his whole body was on fire, and he was glad of the darkness all around. He reached down and sought Thelma's lips with his own, and was rewarded with a kiss as light as a butterfly's wings. Cuddling her close, he shut his eyes and waited for the throbbing desire in his body to cease.

Any possible further manoeuvres were suddenly halted as the film finished and the cinema was illuminated. Dazed and unused to such raw emotions, Neville and Thelma unwillingly broke away from each other, stood up, and made their way to the exit.

"Did you like the film?" Neville was the first to break the silence, and seized the chance to slip his hand in hers again as he walked Thelma back to her car.

"Oh yes, it was great. Did you?" She hoped he didn't ask what bit she liked best. She couldn't even remember what the title was, let alone anything else.

"Yes, it was good. Have you got to go home now then?"

In her mind's eye Thelma could see her mother sitting in the front room, curlers in her hair, looking at the clock with a grim expression, and waiting impatiently for her to come back. Suddenly she didn't care anymore; the throbbing in her nether regions wasn't going away, and she didn't want to go home.

"Well, not just yet. What else did you have in mind?"

"You can come back to my place for coffee if you like? If

you want to drive I'll direct you; it's not far." Neville held his breath.

"Ok."

Neville let his breath out slowly and then kicked himself. Why on earth had he said coffee? He didn't even drink the bloody stuff.

CHAPTER 21

THE BAND WAS too loud, making conversation impossible. Roger was glad to have got Judy away from her brood for the evening (he'd even given the brick shit -house £20 to babysit), but now she seemed more interested in listening to the music. Her head nodded in time to the beat, and her foot tapped out a rhythm on the carpet. This wasn't how he'd envisaged the evening turning out; in the past he'd listened to the bands with his mates and had a bit of a laugh, but now he wanted to talk to this woman and get to know her better. He took a deep breath and raised his voice close to Judy's ear.

"Fancy going on somewhere else a bit quieter?"

Judy was enjoying the music and the evening out. She was finding Roger amusing and good company, but was suddenly wary of getting closer, giving out the wrong signals, and starting up another sexual relationship so soon after her divorce; she owed it to her boys to be careful, so she shook her head and smiled at Roger.

"I'm fine, thanks!"

She raised her voice, and noticed Roger's expression changing to one of disappointment. She could tell he was interested in her, and it made her feel desirable again instead of frumpy and mumsy. Alan had discarded her like an old shoe, and she wondered whether he'd be jealous if Elliott got around to mentioning Roger the next time he visited his father. She hoped so.

"Ok. I'll get another round in!"

Roger disappeared off to the bar, annoyed at Judy's reluctance to leave. He'd have to take her home at the end of the evening, and would have hardly spoken to her properly at all. He would also have to spend another hour or so watching that prick of a singer strutting about in his tight jeans. It had been years since Roger had been able to prise himself into a pair of trousers with a 30 inch waist, and that fact was also pissing him off. Did Judy find the singer more interesting? Roger sipped his beer morosely, and watched Judy out of the corner of his eye. To think that listening to the band had been his idea in the first place……

At 11pm the musicians were directed by the management to switch off the amplifiers, and Roger breathed a sigh of relief.

"I can hear myself think now. That was a bit of a racket!"

"Oh, I enjoyed it. Thanks for the night out." "Fancy a kebab or something like that?"

"Well, I suppose I'd better get back. Brian'll want to start his evening out now."

"Strange. When I was a kid you went to a disco and it finished at midnight or maybe even 1am. Now the clubs don't even open 'till then. I'd be too knackered now to want to go out at midnight." Roger yawned and finished up his beer; "Come on then, let's get you back."

He stopped the car on the access road to the estate.

"Just wanted to check with you if you fancied going out next Saturday?"

"Great. Yes. I'll ask Brian to babysit again and let you know on Monday."

Roger shook his head.

"I don't think I'll go to any more of those classes. I feel a right prat. I just can't do it."

Judy laughed.

"You're fine! Is it helping your shoulder?"

"A bit I suppose, but I can do the shoulder exercises at

home. Those balls kill me."

"Well, it won't be the same without you."

"Here's my mobile number. Send me a text and let me know if next Saturday's ok."

Judy tapped the number into her phone and smiled at Roger as she handed it back:

"I've really enjoyed the night out. Thanks."

"Would you mind very much if I give you a kiss?" Roger surprised himself at his own gentlemanly-ness. Given half the chance he would have jumped her bones..

"If you like." Judy laughed, and her resolve not to get involved with another man so soon began to slip.

His kiss spoke of the passion to come. Judy's response was instant. It had been some time since a man had kissed her at all. They broke away, panting slightly.

"You're a really attractive lady. I don't mind admitting I'm finding it very hard to keep my hands to myself."

"I like you Roger, but I'm no t sure about taking it further just yet. Sorry, but I've been let down once; badly. I owe it to my boys to be sure before I take the next step."

"That's fine. Sorry. I'll drive you home now." At least he was still in with a chance…

He could see the brick shit house watching him through the curtain-less kitchen window.

"I'll look forward to next weekend."

"'Night Roger. Yes, I'll see you soon."

Judy opened the car door, waved goodbye and sighed. Why couldn't there be friendship between a man and a woman without sex getting in the way? He was a nice enough chap though, but with the start of a sexual relationship there would also be the fear of yet another pregnancy. She was 42 and over the hill; another baby would be an absolute disaster. She would have to decide whether to visit the doctor and go back on the pill.

CHAPTER 22

THELMA LEFT A note on the bedside cabinet, tiptoed out of the bedroom, and picked up her bra from where it had fallen at the top of the stairs. Her knickers were somewhere down by the front door. She crept silently downstairs so as not to wake Neville, who was sleeping the sleep of the deeply satiated.

She could hardly believe that she was now no longer a virgin; all those years of keeping her hand on her halfpenny had caused her to miss out on one of life's rich pleasures. Her face burned with the residue of multiple satisfying orgasms. She was going to make up for lost time, but now it was 1.30am and she needed to get dressed; she would be late home and she had to face her mother's anger.

She almost expected to see a police car in the road outside the house as she pulled up into the drive. However, she could see the house was all in darkness except for the flicker-ing of the TV screen through the open curtains of the front room window. Was her mother still watching television? Sylvia usually went to bed at 9.30pm, and for her to still be awake at this hour of the morning was unusual to say the least.

Turning the key quietly in the lock, she let herself in, switched on the light in the hallway, and waited for the barrage of abuse to begin. There was nothing except for the sound of the TV programme. She popped her head around the door of the front room; her mother was fast asleep and sitting up in the armchair in her nightdress, mouth open and snoring.

Thelma washed and changed into her nightclothes, and then returned downstairs to turn off the TV and pull the curtains. She gently shook her mother's shoulder.

"What are you still doing down here Mum? Aren't you coming to bed then?"

Sylvia opened her eyes, dazed and confused.

"When did you come in? I must have fallen asleep. I've been waiting up for you."

"Oh, I came home hours ago. Don't you remember?"

"No, I don't remember at all." She got stiffly to her feet and shuffled upstairs to bed, still half asleep.

Thelma breathed a sigh of relief as she climbed under the duvet. Then the shock hit her like a ton of lead: She had just had passionate, unbridled sex for the last two hours with a man who like her had been too overcome with emotion and the excitement of the moment to even think about using any contraception. She had not taken the pill before, having never had in the past even the hint of a sexual relationship.

Shit!

She was about two weeks into her monthly menstrual cycle.

She closed her eyes and remembered the feel of Neville's body.

It would be ok; it was only the first time. She would take care in the future.

CHAPTER 23

ALICE LINDFORD SIGHED as she tried to do up her boots. The zip didn't seem to go all the way up to the top any more. She straightened up, irritated and red-faced from her efforts. Life sucked. She looked like a little round ball of fat. If only food didn't taste so good, then she wouldn't want to eat it.

She smoothed down her hair and sighed again at the thought of seeing that bloody size zero self-satisfied woman, running along behind her son as he cycled to school. Alice couldn't stand the sight of her; it brought home to her the fact that her weight had almost topped 18 stone, and now she was even getting breathless when bending over and trying to do up her boots. She looked at herself in the mirror; perhaps the time had come to try and shift some of the fat again. She had tried and tried in the past, but dieting had only made her want to eat more.

She let herself out of the 8th floor flat she shared with her daughter, and waited for the lift. Lucy was gaining weight at a fast rate, and Alice knew it wouldn't be long before the kids at school started calling her names. It happened when you were big; there was no escaping from the daily torture.

The top of her legs chafed together as she waddled along the criss-crossing paths that led out of the estate and onto the main road. She was sweating by the time she reached the footpath leading to the school. She hoped that Sandy would be there in the playground to have a chat to, but Carly had been off school and ill for a few days, and Alice hadn't seen her in the playground that morning.

Bugger… there was that woman again, waiting on her own near the entrance gate, rake-thin and perfect.

"Excuse me. Ta."

Alice pushed the gate inwards as Roz stepped out of the way. Bastard! There wasn't a blemish on her body, and her skin was perfect.

"Sorry."

Roz felt the hate emanating from the woman's stare. Why didn't anybody speak to her? What had she done that was so awful? How on earth could she begin to make even one friend?

"I'm Roz, by the way." She smiled and hoped the introduction would break the ice. "What's your name?" If she could just get one of the women to like her, then perhaps all the others would come around in time.

"Alice."

"Pleased to meet you."

"Yeah."

Roz sighed as Alice walked past her and started chatting to one of the other mothers. It was going to be a hard task, but she was determined to make a friend of at least one of them by the end of the term.

CHAPTER 24

"WE SEEM TO be two down tonight."

Petra looked around the room and could only see six people, two of them sitting unnaturally close together.

"Edie's not coming anymore. She told me."

Julian finished shrugging out his shoulders and started stretching his quads. He was really getting into this fitness thing now. Malcolm had been right, as always. Exercise did make you feel better.

"Roger's not coming back either." Judy ignored the inquisitive turning of heads, and lay down on her mat. Let them think what they like…

"Ok, well tonight we're going to ramp it up a bit. Let's all begin by stretching out and warming up those muscles ready to give them a workout. Neville and Thelma, would you like to move your mats a little further apart perhaps?"

As Thelma unwillingly took her gaze from Neville and shifted her mat to the right she was aware that the door had opened and a large lady with obviously dyed bright red shoulder-length hair was talking to Petra, who then waved her in the direction of the stack of exercise mats.

"Get yourself a mat, and find a space. Nice to have you join us. Everyone; this is Alice, who hasn't done Pilates before, but is going to give it a trial tonight."

Roz recognised the woman that she had introduced herself

to in the school playground. She turned around towards the back of the room and called out to where Alice had placed her mat.

"Hi Alice! I'm Roz – remember? I saw you at the school today. I didn't know you were coming here." *Actually you're the last person I would have expected to see at an exercise class…..*

"Hi." *Oh Christ; not Miss Size Zero. That's all I need…* "Ready for the warm up? Let's all stand, shoulders back, navels and pelvic floors pulled in. Big breath in, and then lift the arms up. Exhale as you bring them down slowly. Let's repeat that, and then shrug out the shoulders." Petra wondered if Alice would be back the following week. "Now: big breath in, then lift the arms up and exhale as you bring them down slowly to the same level as your shoulders. Hold the arms there."

Alice's arms were aching already, and her stomach rumbled with hunger. She could see nobody who was as overweight as she was. She wanted to go home. Her mother was looking after Lucy, and she'd probably cooked some lovely fish and chips. The thought of food made her mouth water. She wondered which musical instrument was making the terrible noise coming out of the CD player.

"Let's lift that right arm up and over the head, then do the same with the left arm; four to each side. Keep the navel pulled in and the pelvic floor up."

Roz wondered how Alice was getting on next to Judy at the back; she couldn't hear them talki ng. The two lovebirds were in the front, gazing at each other like sick cows, and Julian and Malcolm were alongside her in the middle row. Perhaps they'd be able to chat in the queue for water?

"Let's roll down slowly. Keep the navel pulled in and let the arms hang, just as though somebody had draped you over a washing line."

God, this was torture! Alice tried to bend in the middle, but her stomach was in the way. She stood up, unable to carry on. Roz seemed to have folded herself in two like a piece of paper, and Alice hated the sight of her.

"Now come up slowly and then grab some weights from the box. We're going to do some bicep curls and shoulder presses."

Alice took the lightest weights she could find and decided to copy the two obviously gay men in front of her. At least she might be able to do this one…

Petra changed the CD, and Alice recognised the strains of 'Stayin' Alive' echoing around the room.

"Hold a weight in each hand, palms facing inwards. Now push the right arm up to the ceiling and then the left. Come on; work it! Eight presses with each arm and then another eight!"

Up went the arms in time to Barry Gibb's falsetto.

"Now keep the elbows in close to the body and curl the right hand to shoulder height and then down again. Do the same with the left for a series of eight curls with each arm."

Barry was giving it his all as Petra worked the class to a fine sweat.

"Are you all warmed up? Now find a space next to the wall. Don't forget those navels should be pulled in. Press your back against the wall, but bring your feet out a little bit away and put them hip distance apart."

Alice wondered what was coming next. She wasn't long in finding out.

"Slide your back down the wall and pretend you're sitting on a chair." Alice thought Petra seemed to be enjoying herself over the howls of protestations coming from the woman who'd been on the mat next to her and the couple who seemed to need surgically removing from each other. Only Roz and the two gays sat still on their invisible chairs; calm and comfortable. Alice wanted to kill them. She couldn't even begin to do this one; her legs were just too weak.

Julian felt good as he sat with his legs bent and his back against the wall; he felt strong and supple. He turned his head to the side and grinned at Malcolm; he could sit like this all day. Malcolm returned his grin.

Life was good!

CHAPTER 25

THELMA WAS SHELVING the returned fiction books when she suddenly felt her stomach heave and lurch. She had to drop the books and run to the toilet, ejecting her break-time cup of tea and three digestive biscuits.

Kneeling over the toilet bowl until the waves of nausea had decreased, she tried to think of what she'd eaten that might have upset her digestive system so much. Her mother had cooked a lovely lamb casserole the night before, buy she had skipped breakfast that morning because she hadn't felt hungry. Maybe the lamb had been off?

Feeling weak but a bit better, Thelma got shakily to her feet, flushed the toilet, and sat down on the seat to recover.

It couldn't be the contraceptive pill that was making her sick, as she hadn't even started taking it yet. She was keeping Neville at arm's length and waiting until after her next period so that she could start it properly, as per the instructions. Funnily enough though, her period was taking longer than usual to arrive.

Thelma stood up slowly and went to the sink to rinse her mouth. She could still taste the digestive biscuits. She never wanted to eat another one again.

"Are you ok? You look a bit pale." Anne's face was a picture of consternation as she opened the door.

"I've just thrown up. Can't think what could have caused it though."

"Well, at least it's not morning sickness! I threw up day after day when I was having my two. You must have eaten something bad." Anne looked at the prematurely dried-up spinster in front of her and wondered if she'd ever even been kissed at all. "Go off home. We're not busy. It'll be ok."

"Thanks. I feel rather peculiar. I'll check how Mum is when I get home. I'll see you tomorrow."

Pulling up onto the driveway, Thelma still felt slightly nauseous and her breasts were unusually sore and heavy. She waved to her mother who was weeding in the front garden.

"You're home early! What's wrong?" Sylvia put down her hoe and walked over to the car.

"I've been sick. Were you ok after last night's dinner?"

"I'm as right as rain. I've been weeding the flowerbeds. Go upstairs and have a lie down. You'll feel better after a sleep."

Her mother was right. Thelma felt fine after an hour's doze, and was ready for some lunch. She even wondered about going back to the library for the afternoon, but thought she'd better stay at home in case she felt sick again. However, the lunch stayed in her stomach, and afterwards she joined her mother out in the garden, revelling in the warm sunshine and the chance to sit on a chair and read her book.

She suddenly wondered if Neville had called in to the library at lunchtime to change his books. She decided to send him a text to explain her absence, in case he'd been looking for her. Within a few moments of sending the text there was an answering ping.

'Sorry to hear you're not well. Let me know when you're feeling better and we can carry on where we left off … xxx'

She felt a warm throb in her nether regions at the thought of carrying on with Neville where they'd left off. Her period was due any day now, and when that was over with she would take her first pill and look forward to awakening a part of her that had been dormant for too long.

However, the smell of Anne's coffee in the little library kitchenette the next morning made her stomach heave again, and she only just made it to the toilet before jettisoning her breakfast. She began to feel worried; her period still hadn't arrived, and her breasts were so sore that there was no way Neville was going to be allowed to get anywhere near them.

She started to catastrophise; surely she couldn't be pregnant? They'd only had sex the one time; granted that it had gone on for two wonderful hours, but no, she couldn't be; she mustn't be. Whatever would her mother, the family and her work colleagues say? What would Neville say? She shuddered with horror; she would give her period another few days to arrive and if it didn't appear she would have to go back to the doctor, although she was sure that wouldn't be necessary.

CHAPTER 26

THELMA KEPT HER gaze fixed on the ceiling. Her face burned with embarrassment as the doctor's fingers probed her most intimate places. She sighed with some degree of relief as the examination came to an end and she could bring her knees back together again.

"My examination agrees with the results of your urine test Miss Frost; you're about two months' pregnant. A scan in a few weeks' time will give us a more accurate due date."

Oh my God, no! Whatever was she going to say to Neville and her mother?

"Are you absolutely sure, doctor?" She clung on to a last minute hope that the GP had somehow made a terrible mistake.

"Certain as certain can be. Congratulations. You're going to be a mother!"

Thelma stepped blindly out into the late afternoon sunshine of the high street, looking with envy at people going by leading their normal lives while she was shaking with nervousness at the conversation she knew would have to take place as soon as she returned home. Neville would be also be sending her a text sooner or later making sure she was going to Pilates that evening; she would have to decline, she just couldn't think about Pilates any more. Her whole orderly world was starting to crumble around the edges.

Opening the car door, she sat down heavily on the seat and burst into tears. How could this have happened to her, a modest, quiet librarian? She'd only had sex once! She'd been so careful these past weeks not to allow herself to get pregnant. Would she still be able to do her job (she could just imagine all the gossip at the library)? She was so tired now, all the time; a mind-numbing tiredness that wouldn't go away. She just wanted to go to sleep and forget about it all…

Drying her eyes and feeling better for the release of emotion, she started up the car and moved off slowly towards home.

"Is that you Thelma?" Her mother's shrill voice called out over the noise of the TV.

Who else would it be?

"Yes Mum, it's me."

"What did the doctor say? Do you need a tonic or something?" Sylvia came out into the hallway, a concerned look upon her face.

"Oh Mum, it's terrible!" The tears began again as Thelma crumpled up into a heap on the stairs, sobbing.

"Whatever's the matter? Tell me!" Sylvia began to panic; her daughter was usually so calm and in control of herself.

Thelma's sobs grew louder:

"Mum, I'm pregnant!"

Sylvia looked aghast:

"But you can't be! You've never even had a boyfriend!"

Thelma took a deep breath and tried to regain her composure.

"Yes I have got a boyfriend. It's just that I haven't told you about him."

"Who is he? Why have you kept him a secret? Will you be moving in with him then? What's going to happen to me?" Sylvia started to tremble at the implications.

"I don't know anything at the moment. I haven't even told him yet. I'm still coming to terms with it myself." Thelma closed her eyes and put one side of her head against the cool wall. She heard the phone buzz in her handbag with an incoming text.

"Thank goodness your father's not alive to see the shame of it all. You, a single mother; after all my efforts to bring you up properly!"

"Oh Mum, there's no shame in it anymore! It's not the 1950's. I've got to go and see Neville now and talk to him." She stood up, desperately tired but suddenly wanting to be away as far as she could from her mother.

"But you haven't had any tea yet!" "I
don't want any. I'll be back later."

Thelma virtually ran out of the front door and got back in the car. She had to see Neville and tell him. She couldn't send an answering text; it just wouldn't be right.

Neville checked his watch and then his mobile phone again. It was unlike Thelma not to have answered his text; he would give her a call.

The number was dialling up when he heard a noise outside. Going over to the window he saw Thelma getting out of her car, slamming the door, and running up the front path. She didn't look as though she was dressed for Pilates. He wondered if she was ill and had come round to tell him she wasn't going.

When he opened the front door a small tornado flew sobbing into his arms; he was almost knocked back by the force. He gently drew her into the hallway and out of sight of any nosey neighbours. Closing the door quickly he held her tight and waited until her weeping had subsided.

"Are you going to tell me what's wrong?"

"Oh Neville...I – I'm pregnant!" Thelma knew she'd lose him now; who'd want to be tied down to her and a baby?

Neville held her at arm's length and looked into her eyes. He smiled.

"That's wonderful news! Why are you crying?" "B-Because
we've only known each other a short time and
I thought you wouldn't be interested." She wiped her eyes
and hoped against hope that he wasn't going to run a mile.

"How could I not be interested in my own child? I'm not

far off forty years of age; it's about time I became a father!"
He kissed her and heard her exhale softly; "We'll be a proper
family; you, me and the baby. There's no way I'm ever going
to let you go now."

They stood embracing for some time. Finally Neville
broke free and cupped Thelma's chin with his hand.

"Anyway. There's one advantage to all this."

"What's that?"

"We can have as much sex as we like. We won't have any
worries about you getting pregnant!"

Thelma laughed through her tears:

"Do you want to go to Pilates tonight?"

"I'd rather do some horizontal jogging and go to bed with
you."

As they took off their clothes and looked at each other,
Thelma remembered just in time to switch off her mobile
phone for the evening.

CHAPTER 27

ROGER WAS WAITING for Judy in the car outside the leisure centre. She smiled at him as she opened the passenger door.

"There were only five of us there tonight. No sign of Thelma and Neville. I think they've hit it off actually; they've been as close as close could be."

Roger started up the car. Lucky old them…

"What? The merchant banker and the one that looks like she's sat on a wasp's nest? There's a match made in heaven…."

"Don't take the piss. They looked very happy last week."

"Well, good for them. You never know, there's always the chance that perhaps we could follow suit?"

Roger held his breath as he pulled away from the kerb, and then exhaled as he summoned up courage.

"I've been thinking."

"What about?"

"Well, about us."

"Us? I didn't know we were actually a couple. I thought we were just friends." Judy's stomach started to tighten in knots. She had a distinct feeling that she knew exactly what Roger was going to say.

Roger kept a steady gaze on the road ahead.

"Well, we are. We've had a few good nights out now, so I

wondered how you felt about a weekend away somewhere nice?"

The implications of this statement were not lost on Judy, and she took a few moments to think it over. In the silence that followed she came to the conclusion that in a few short years she would be pushing 50, and her chances for happiness might possibly start to decline. She smiled and turned towards Roger.

"That sounds great. I'll check with Alan when he's free so that Elliott and Marlon can visit for the weekend. Where were you thinking of going then?"

Roger momentarily closed his eyes in relief; he'd even go to hell in a handcart for the weekend, just as long as he could go there with Judy:

"You choose. I'll only pick somewhere awful. You book it up and I'll drive us there; double or single rooms, whatever you like. Deal?"

"Deal. Judy laughed as the car turned onto the estate. She would definitely go back on the pill…

"D'you want to come in for coffee, if you can stand the kids?"

"Course I do. I'm getting to like them."

"Really?"

"Yeah, really. Your Brian's a laugh a minute."

Judy wasn't sure if he was joking or not as she got out of the car.

"Hi Mum."

Roger noticed Elliott giving him the evil eye as he walked past the boy, who was standing in the garden with some friends.

"Have you done your homework?" Judy looked back over her shoulder towards her youngest son before walking through the open front door.

"We weren't set any."

"That's what you said yesterday."

"We weren't set any then either."

"Alright?" Roger nodded to Brian, who brushed past him in the passage on his way out.

"Ok. Mum, can I have that tenner now? I'm meeting Shaz in the pub."

"Didn't I give it to you before I went out?"

"No, and I'm skint."

Judy fished in her purse.

"Here's two fivers. Can you go up to Marlon and ask him to turn the music down on your way out please."

"Ta. Will do."

"Where's Nick?"

"Out with Lisa."

"What's happened to Tracey?"

"He dumped her."

"Why?"

"She wanted his babies."

Judy looked at Roger and sighed as she switched on the kettle:

"Do you really want to get mixed up with all us lot?"

"I'm up for it if you are."

"You can do better."

"I'll let you know after our weekend away."

"Cheeky sod!"

She started to give him a playful punch, but Roger caught her wrist and drew her towards him, and they kissed for what seemed to Judy like an eternity. Finally she broke away when she heard Marlon's footsteps coming down the stairs.

"I'll book a double if that's ok with you?"

"I was hoping you'd say that."

CHAPTER 28

"SLOW DOWN! Mummy can't keep up!"

Roz pounded along the pavement as fast as she could, keeping an eye on Jimmy as he pedalled furiously along in front. Not too far ahead she could see the usual group of mothers and children walking to school along the footpath; she recognised Alice's red hair in the midst of the group, who was holding the hand of an equally flame-haired small girl.

She decided it was now or never.

"Morning Alice!" Roz panted as she ran past; "Going to Pilates tonight?"

"Yeah. I lost two pounds last week!" Alice laughed and waved.

"Good for you!"

Roz felt uplifted at receiving a response. She hung about near the gate after Jimmy had padlocked his bike instead of jogging back straightaway, waiting for Alice to reappear.

"How d'you do that bloody chair exercise? I could hardly walk the next day!" Alice sighed as she walked past the gate on her way home.

Roz decided to walk along slowly beside her:

"I couldn't do it at first either. They used to make me do it at kickboxing. I suppose my legs have got used to it."

"You're a bloody marvel, you are. Whatever you're on, I want some." Alice sighed at the thought of having to lose half her body weight. She was starving hungry already, and it was only 09:15.

It was time for Roz to stick her neck out even further.

"I've made some lovely rice cakes. You can come back now and try one with a quick cup of tea if you like. I'm only a couple of streets away."

"Ok. That sounds great. Better than going back home to tidy up my flat anyway!" The sound of the word 'cake' was too tempting for Alice to ignore.

Even though it was early morning, the house was pristine. Alice had never seen anything like it. Everything was in its place, tidy and neat. She couldn't see any evidence that a little boy lived there at all.

"Wow! What a lovely house!" Alice looked around appreciatively. "My flat's a mess. Lucy's stuff is all over the place."

"Oh, you should have seen it this morning when I got up. I can't go out unless I know the house is
    tidy." "What time do you get up then?"

"5.30. I like to clean around before Jimmy gets up."

"What about your husband? Are you hoovering around him in the bed then?" Alice laughed at the sudden mental image."

"He has to get up early for work. We're all early birds here."

Roz filled the kettle and wiped some drips of water up on the work surface with a cloth.

"What do you like to drink? I've got green tea, decaffeinated ordinary teabags, all manner of fruit teas, or coffee. Mark, my partner, likes coffee, but I don't drink it."

Alice had never heard of green tea, but wondered whether to try some.

"I usually drink coffee, but I think I'll try your green tea. I'm curious now." She hoped she hadn't made a bad choice, but if it helped her to lose excess fat and end up looking like Roz then she was all for it.

"It's very good for you. It helps to neutralise any free radicals in your diet. That's the stuff that causes cancer." Roz poured boiling water onto a green teabag and let it stew for a moment. "I've made these rice cakes to go with it." She opened a tin, indicating to Alice to take one. "Jimmy loves them."

Alice looked in the tin and saw clusters of Rice Krispies stuck together with something unknown. She would usually have had a slice or two of chocolate Swiss roll by now. She sipped her green tea, shuddered, and assumed pond weed would taste better. The rice cake didn't even touch the sides; she could have eaten all the cakes in the tin, but they didn't seem to taste of anything in particular.

"How have you got so much energy? I envy you." Alice was ashamed to admit that she sometimes went back to bed for the whole morning after she'd taken Lucy to school.

"I haven't always been like this. I once weighed 12 stones at the time of leaving home, but soon lost weight when I started eating sensibly and exercising." Roz had never admitted this to anybody before; not even Mark knew.

"Wow. I'd be happy to weigh even 12 stones." Alice felt like crying at the mountain she had to climb.

"It's a question of educating your taste buds to expect less sugar. It's sugar that makes you feel tired." Roz decided not to mention the terrible craving for sweet foods that she'd had to start with. She'd nearly packed it all in after a couple of weeks and given in to cherry scones with jam and cream when on holiday in Cornwall. "After about a month your brain gets used to less sugar, and anything sweet tastes sickly."

"I hope so. It's doing my head in at the moment."

"I'd be happy to pass on some recipes." "Thanks. Thanks very much."

Alice felt more hopeful as she walked back to her flat. Perhaps she could learn something from this whirling dervish?

As Roz washed up the cups she wondered if she had found a friend at last.

CHAPTER 29

JULIAN FELT UNEASY as he rolled the gym ball towards his mat. Malcolm hadn't come home until after 2am on Sunday morning, and on Sunday night he hadn't come home at all. His explanation hadn't been convincing, and now he was missing from the Pilates class. Julian sighed and looked towards the door; he'd felt certain his boyfriend would have been there that evening. He wondered if he'd been dumped for the good-looking, black haired, well-muscled boy at the gym whom he'd often seen Malcolm giving surreptitious looks to lately.

If only he could find a way to halt the steady march of time! He had slid into middle age silently and without a whimper, accepting of his fate. How could he make his 42-year-old body look 22 again? That was the age-old problem; he couldn't, and now Malcolm's eye was wandering. No amount of hair dye or cosmetic surgery was going to solve the problem.

Petra noticed that Julian seemed to have lost his usual sparkle. He sat on his ball, morose and silent. She put a relaxation disc into the CD player, looked around the room, and came over to stand in front of the class.

"Good evening everyone! I'm glad you enjoyed the class enough to come back again, Alice."

"I don't know about enjoying it, but I'm doing it."

"That's the spirit. Keep it up and you'll see the results. Now let's begin with our usual stretches and warm up exercises. Stay sitting on your gym balls and let's move the hips round and round; first one way and then the other. Pretend you're in Hawaii doing the hula-hula dance."

Alice wondered whether her gym ball would explode due to the pressure it was under. She moved her hips around tentatively, noticing that the gay-looking chap in front of her didn't seem to be moving at all; he was sitting still and looking at the floor. Suddenly she saw him stand up, collect his bag and coat and walk out. She looked towards Petra, who shrugged her shoulders.

"Sit up tall on your balls with your navel and pelvic floor pulled well in. We seem to have been reducing in numbers over the last couple of weeks. I don't think I'll be allowed to continue unless there's at least six people, but we shall see." Petra knew something like this would happen, it always did; one by one they would drop out for one reason or another. The powers-that-be should have made them all pay up front for all the lessons, instead of pay-on-the-night. It was always a recipe for disaster.

Alice sighed as her endomorphic body habitus protested against being flung about on a gym ball. She had just found an exercise class that she felt reasonably comfortable with, and now it looked as though everyone was dropping out. Would she ever be able to lose any weight?

CHAPTER 30

JULIAN TOOK ANOTHER swig from the bottle of Jack Daniels and breathed in the dank air as he stood waiting on the platform for the train, glad of the anonymity of London Bridge underground station. Everywhere tourists and commuters scurried to and fro around him going about their business, or going home to loved ones. Nobody gave him a second glance.

He gazed enviously at the back of the young man standing in front of him; he had youth and vitality on his side. No amount of whisky could dull that fact that Julian had neither, and would never have either one again. He fingered Malcolm's letter in his pocket. There were still a few minutes left to re -read it, just to make sure he had got it right the first time.

'Dear Jules,

I'm so sorry it has to be this way. I can't ignore my feelings for Rick, and it wouldn't be fair to string you along. I couldn't face a scene when you came home from work. I've taken all my stuff, taken some unpaid leave, and we're staying with one of Rick's friends in a flat in London for the time being, but will probably still live in Norwich eventually. It's probably best if I don't give you the address just yet. I hope we can still be friends. We had some good times. Thanks for the memories, love Malcolm. X'

So that was his name, Rick; owner of the black wavy hair

and bulging biceps. Bastard!

The amber liquid burned his throat as Julian drank down past the label. There was nothing left; he was 42, middle-aged and a has-been, a sad old queen with nothing to fill his time except to remember his youth and what used to be. The days stretched endlessly before him, dark and dreary, just consisting of creating cauliflowers for elderly ladies who were just as lonely as himself. One day he would be as old as them, with blue-veined parchment-like skin, thin hair and brittle bones. He would pick up the hairdryer, and its weight would cause his frail body to crumble into dust....

He couldn't stop the tears. Nobody was watching, so he let them fall.

A rush of air signalled the approaching tube train. He never thought it would ever come to this; what a way to go! He could just see the headlines in tomorrow's tabloids: Queer death on the Northern Line (or should it be Queer's Death on the Northern Line?).

Julian dropped the whisky, and pushed forward past the young man, who looked around momentarily as the glass bottle smashed to the ground, spilling its contents. There was just enough time to jump before the train reached the station...

He reached the edge of the platform, closed his eyes and took a deep breath, working up enough courage to launch himself onto the rails and the sweet release from all the sadness and pain.

"It's all right, mate. I've got you." A deep voice sounded in his ear, and Julian felt somebody holding onto the back of his coat.

This was not supposed to happen!

"Leave me alone! I want to die!"

Julian, desperate now, tried to disentangle himself from the man's grip as the train slowly slid to a halt. The doors opened and passengers rushed either side of them to the exit, unconcerned and unknowing of the drama taking place before them.

"No you don't. You wouldn't have hesitated. If you were serious you would have jumped and I'd never have been able to catch you."

"What do you know?"

"In my job I've seen it all, mate." The man looked down. "Anyway, you owe me now. Look what you've done; I've got whisky all over my shoes, and it's all your fault."

Julian opened his eyes to see the young man he had noticed earlier. However, he looked somehow younger from the back than he did from the front.

"Go away! Piss off! What business is it of yours? Catch your train; leave me alone, you bastard!" The whisky was beginning to take effect, and Julian swayed with the effort of remaining upright.

"No way. You're coming home with me. You'll thank me later. Get on the bloody train."

Julian felt himself being manhandled aboard the tube. He sank gratefully down onto a seat, shaking and dizzy. Waves of nausea washed over him.

"I'm going to throw up." He stood up again and staggered out onto the station, followed by the man. The doors closed and the train moved off. Julian expelled his stomach contents onto the platform, oblivious to the looks of disgust from the waiting passengers.

"Now I've got sick all over my shoes as well. You definitely owe me now."

"Take all my fucking money and buy yourself a shoe shop."

"Yeah, I will. In the meantime we're still getting on the next train though and you're coming home with me. We've got another ten minutes to wait."

The man steered Julian over towards an empty seat and they sat down. Julian leaned forward and put his head in his hands as another wave of nausea overcame him. Travellers moved away from the two men as Julian retched and heaved.

"You'll feel like the inside of a soap-boiler's arsehole in the morning, turned inside out and whitewashed, as my old Nan used to say. You must have drunk nearly the whole bottle."

"Go away. Go away."

"Shut up. I've saved your life and you haven't even asked me what my name is."

"I don't care what your name is."

"There's gratitude for you. It's Simon, by the way. What's yours?"

"Julian."

"Nice to meet you Julian …. I think."

CHAPTER 31

HE HAD NO idea where he was or how he got there; his head hurt, and his mouth felt like the bottom of a parrot's cage. He could still taste whisky; he felt as though he never wanted to drink it ever again. Julian opened his eyes and looked around; he seemed to be lying on somebody's sofa under a thin blanket. He looked under the blanket to find he was dressed in only his underpants.

"Morning! Or should I say afternoon, seeing as it's just gone past mid-day?"

"Who are you? Where is this?" Julian struggled to sit up, screwing up his eyes at the light from the fluorescent bulb overhead.

"I'm the one that saved your life; remember? I'm Simon with the shoes covered in whisky and sick. Here; I've made you a cup of tea."

Julian took the proffered cup, took a sip of hot tea, and then put the cup down on the floor. He flopped back on the cushion and closed his eyes. It was all coming back to him like a bad dream; well, some of it anyway.

"Where is this?" Where am I?"

"I live not far London Bridge station. I work as a Charge Nurse at Guy's. This is my flat, for what it's worth. Where do you live?"

"Nowhere near here. I live in Norfolk. I work as a hairdresser. I guess my cauliflowers will be wondering where I am today."

Simon laughed.

"What the hell were you doing on the tube station last night then?"

"My friend moved to London temporarily. I came down on the train to try and find him."

"London's a big place. What part?"

"I don't know. I tried to call him when I got here but he'd switched his phone off."

Julian felt dreadful, sick and weary. He wanted to go home, creep under his duvet, and sleep for a week. He felt ashamed of all the trouble he'd caused to this man, a complete stranger who had gone out of his way to help him.

"I've got a day off today. If you like, we can go out and get some lunch, but take a shower first, I can smell you from here."

Julian felt tears pricking the back of his eyes.

"Thanks so much, Simon. I'm sorry for being such an arsehole yesterday."

"Hey, it's not a problem."

"Where are my clothes? Any idea?"

"I put them on the quick wash this morning. They're going round in the tumble drier."

By the time he had showered, shaved and dressed he was feeling somewhat better, although little men with pickaxes were still hammering around inside his head. Julian followed Simon out of the flat and into the bright light of day, wishing he had brought his sunglasses.

"Still hung over?"

"Yeah."

"I know a great café near London Bridge. It's built into the railway arches. You can get a lovely bacon roll in there. It's like a big doorstep; all greasy and buttery."

"Just…..don't. Alright?"

"Only joking."
"I just want a cup of coffee and a slice of toast."

CHAPTER 32

"DAD AND CARA are going to take you both to the cinema and then out for dinner tonight, and then somewhere nice tomorrow; probably to the seaside maybe."

"Where are you going?" Elliott finished up the last of his cereal: "Is there any more of this?"

"No, but there's fruit or yoghurt if you like. Roger and I will be having a weekend away. I'll be back tomorrow evening."

"Will you be sleeping with him then?"

"Marlon – that's none of your business. Roger is a good friend."

"But is he your boyfriend?"

"Not at the moment, but we'll see. Now eat up. Dad will be here to pick you up soon."

"Hey Dad!"

Judy thought Elliott seemed quite pleased to see his father. Thank goodness there was no sign of Cara.

"Alright?" Judy could see Alan looking about in the hope of seeing Brian or Nick, but she had suggested in the interests of peace they made themselves scarce. "Where's Marlon?" "He's gone back up to his room. I'll give him a shout."

Judy opened up the bedroom door.

"Dad's here, Marlon."

"He's a wanker."

"Don't say that. He's your father and he loves you."

"Oh yeah, 'course he does." "Come on; he's waiting."

"I don't want to go. I'm staying here with Brian and Nick."

She sighed as she returned downstairs.

"He doesn't want to go. He wants to stay here."

"Shall I go up?"

"No. You and Elliott go. Marlon will be fine. The boys will keep an eye on him."

"When will you be back then?"

"Tomorrow evening. Bring Elliott back after 6 o'clock please."

"Bye Mum!" Judy thought Elliott looked pleased to have his father all to himself.

"See you soon. Be good."

"Has that bastard gone now?" Brian opened his bedroom door and shouted over the landing banisters.

"Yes, but Marlon's still here. He wants to stay with you and Nick."

"Oh, Christ. That's all I need. Shaz is coming over to-night."

"I never worked out if Shaz is male or female?" "Female."

"I'm sure he won't be any trouble, and there's plenty of food in the fridge for you all. Just make sure he's not sitting at that computer until all hours of the morning."

"It'll cost you." Brian came downstairs to where Judy stood in the hallway. "Twenty quid should do it."

"Haven't you just been paid?" Judy searched in her handbag for her purse.

"Yeah, but I'm skint."

"What are you spending it on?"

"Don't know. It just goes."

"Where's Nick? Roger will be here soon, and I wanted to say goodbye."

"Round Dionne's house."

"What's happened to Lisa?"

"Don't ask."

"Oh."

Judy heard the doorbell ring and Brian talking to Roger as she finished packing. She popped her head around the door of Marlon's room:

"I'm off now. See you tomorrow. Ok?"

"I'm fine Mum. Don't worry." Marlon's fingers were flying over the keyboard.

"No computering, Twittering and Googling all night."

"OK."

She saw Roger look up and smile as she came down the stairs.

"All ready?"

"Yes, but Marlon didn't want to go with his father."

"He'll be ok, Mum. Go and have a good weekend."

"Thanks Bri. See you tomorrow." "Look after her, Roger."

"Absolutely."

Judy tried to put her worries behind her as she slid into the passenger seat of Roger's car.

"I hope Brian checks that Marlon's not sitting at that computer all night. I'd rather he was out with his mates, but he's quiet, that one. He doesn't have many friends. It's the quiet ones you've got to watch."

"Didn't you put the parental lock on it?"

"Yes, the Net Nanny's on, but I wonder if he knows how to get around it. Do you think he does?"

"I'm afraid I don't know. I only know how to do the basics."

"Where are you taking me then?" Roger put the car in gear and pulled away from the kerb.

"I've booked us a B&B in Sandbright. I know it's still early in the year, but there's a lovely sandy beach, and loads of shops and amusements. We used to take the boys there way back when."

"Sandbright beach it is then."

Judy crossed her legs, sat back in the seat, and wondered what the evening would bring.

CHAPTER 33

JULIAN FINISHED THE last crumb of toast and drank the rest of his coffee. He was relieved to feel slightly better than he had on waking up. He tried not to let negative thoughts of Malcolm run riot through his head and make him any more depressed than he was already.

"All done? Told you it's a good café." Simon smiled and fished in his pocket for some change.

"No, I'll get it. I owe you big time." Julian stood up and started walking over to the counter.

"I already told you, it's no problem. Just glad I was there to be of service."

Stepping out of the café, Julian looked at his watch.

"I'd best be getting back home. I'm supposed to be at work."

"How about a quick walk along the Embankment? It's a lovely afternoon, and you won't be home in time to go back to work anyway."

"Yeah, ok."

They crossed Tooley Street and walked down to the Embankment, dodging tourists carrying expensive-looking cameras who were making their way to London Bridge station or for sightseeing at the Shard. Julian made his way to an empty seat and sank down, enjoying the cool fresh air on his face and the view of the Thames.

"Can't beat London, eh? The river; I love it. I could watch the boats going up and down all day." Simon turned to Julian, sitting quietly beside him.

"I don't get down to London much."

"You should. I know some great clubs."

"Yeah, well I'm gay."

"So am I. So what? As I said, I know some great clubs."

"Have you got a partner? How would he feel about me stringing along?"

"There's no-one special. How about you?"

"Malcolm and I had been together a couple of years. I got a 'Dear John' note, or rather a 'Dear Julian' note last week."

"Hence your teetering presence on the edge of the platform."

"How did you know I was thinking of jumping then?"

"I'm psychic."

"Yeah?"

"Yeah. And you looked a bit desperate."

"Sorry for the dramatics."

"That's ok. I got to do my Good Samaritan impression."

A hint of a smile crossed Julian's pale features.

"So you know some great clubs, eh?"

"Bloody right I do. And I'm on a late shift tomorrow. We can hit the clubs tonight and you can crash on my sofa again if you like."

"That might be just what I need. But I know one thing." "What?"

"I definitely won't be drinking any more whisky."

CHAPTER 34

ROGER OPENED THE car door and looked out at their accommodation. If it had been anybody else other than Judy that he was sharing a room with he would have cancelled the booking straight away. However, he didn't want to be seen making a fuss.

"Where did you find this place?"

"On the Internet. It's cheap and cheerful."

"It's cheap all right; look at the state of it! All the paint's peeling on the window frames." Roger frowned at the noise of barking dogs and a screaming child coming from the house on the opposite side of the road.

"It's only for one night. Come on, let's go inside."

"I hope I can still see the car from the bedroom window."

"It's not that bad. Stop moaning."

Carrying the bags and grumbling, Roger locked the car and followed Judy up to the reception desk.

"Good afternoon, have you booked?" The elderly, obese landlady smiled through yellowed teeth.

"Yes, a double room in the name of Judy Barr." Judy tried to ignore the waft of stale cabbage emanating from somewhere down the hallway.

"You're in room four on the first floor; I'll show you." The landlady climbed the stairs with some difficulty, pausing on the upstairs landing to catch her breath and to point at a room at the end of the passage:

"There's the bathroom and toilet. Be careful not to let the shower overflow, or water will drip down onto my dining table below." She gave a raspy cough, "And look out for the hibernating butterflies; we always get them this time every year." She turned the key in a lock before passing it to Roger. "Here's your room."

As the landlady wheezed and waddled downstairs again, Judy tried hard not to giggle. On first sight of their bedroom her heart sank to see a small, old-fashioned type of wooden double bed with a definite sag in the middle, covered by a thin 1950's-type candlewick bedspread of an uncertain mustard colour. A grimy mirror hung above a cracked, stained enamel sink in one corner, and the rest of the room she could see was taken up with an old wooden tallboy and two faded chintz armchairs oozing stuffing.

"Good God. I've never seen anything like it!" Roger's head swivelled from side to side in disbelief.

"It's only for one night. Let's make the most of it." Ju-dy's feigned jollity belied a rapidly increasing depression.

"If I get in that bed there'll be no room for you. Look at the size of me; you'll be hanging out over the edge!"

However, Roger suddenly had an agreeable thought that their enforced togetherness could actually work to his advantage, and decided to go along with Judy's plan.

"Oh all right, it can't be as bad as all that, surely?

"That's the spirit! I've been camping with four boys in the rain, and this is miles better than a tent in a muddy field." Judy looked around again and briefly wondered how on earth it could have been listed on the Internet as three-star accommodation.

"I'll take your word for that." Roger threw the bags down onto one of the armchairs. The action caused a fine layer of dust to billow forth, which settled down onto an old rag rug covering a small square of scuffed, varnished floorboards.

"I'm going to check out the shower before we go out for dinner."

"Look out for the hibernating butterflies." Roger sank down onto the bed with a sigh, closed his eyes, and listened to the bedsprings creaking out a howl of protest. Within a few short minutes Judy was back.

"That's it. I'm not staying here. Let's find somewhere else." She began to put on her shoes and coat.

"What's wrong?" Roger sat up on the bed with difficulty.

"There are somebody's hairs in the bottom of the shower. They're short and curly."

CHAPTER 35

ROGER AWOKE TO the smell of freshly percolated coffee. He opened his eyes to see the agreeable vision of Judy pottering about their hotel suite dressed only in his shirt.

"Come back to bed for a cuddle."

"I'm making some coffee first." Judy threw him a shy smile.

"It's only half past eight."

"I can't help it. I'm always up early, even on Sundays." She handed Roger a steaming cup and climbed back under-neath the duvet."

"I could get used to this." He took a sip of the scalding liquid before placing his cup on the bedside table. "You look great in my shirt. You'd look even better without it though." He started to undo the buttons.

"I've had four babies; I'm covered in stretch marks."

"Bollocks to that. Look what your body's doing to me."

Judy laughed and could see that he was already erect. She liked this rough-and-ready builder, and felt good about the effect she was having on him. She never thought any man would want to start a relationship with a mother of four teenage boys.

"I don't want to let you go, now that I've found you." He removed the shirt, flung it on the floor, and Judy enjoyed the feeling of his warm hands as they touched her breasts. "Last night was special."

"I like you, Roger. I like you a lot. You've got no airs and graces; just like me."

"Yep. I'm a fine example of an uncouth, fat bastard."

"You're not fat, just well-covered." Judy laid herself on top of him, "And only a little bit uncouth. And you're definitely not a bastard."

"I think I love you, Jude." His arms went around her and his lips sought hers.

The sound of her phone buzzing on the bedside cabinet brought Judy down to earth. Reluctantly she pulled away and reached over to pick it up.

"Leave it." Roger gave a *tut* of annoyance.

"I can't. There might be something wrong at home."

She looked at the iPhone screen and grimaced.

"What do you want, Alan?"

"Sorry it's early, but I thought I'd better let you know." Her ex-husband's voice on the other end of the line sounded cool and confident.

"Know what?" Judy started to panic as a thousand possibilities flew around in her head.

"It's Elliott. He doesn't want to come home."

"Of course he does. He can't stay with you; you're at work all day."

"Cara only works part-time three days a week; she's home by 2 o'clock."

Judy's anger knew no bounds.

"Listen here – she's got my husband, but I'm fucking certain she's not having my son as well. He comes home tonight or I'll go to the courts."

"Don't be unreasonable. He says he doesn't like the food you're giving him now, and he especially doesn't like your new boyfriend."

"Alan; I'll say this one more time. He comes home at 6 o'clock tonight or I'm going to the courts. Put Elliott on the line."

"He doesn't want to speak to you."

"What's going on Jude?" Roger had reluctantly put the idea of another session of lovemaking to the back of his mind.

"Is that the new boyfriend I can hear? Staying over now is he?" Alan's voice had taken on a tone of contempt.

"What business is it of yours? You're hardly whiter than white in that department yourself. Who had an affair with Miss Tits and Arse? Who left his wife and four sons?"

Shaking and distressed, Judy decided to end the conversation. She put the phone back on the bedside cabinet and cuddled up to Roger.

"I'm sorry. He makes me so angry. I thought he'd try this sooner or later. He's pissed off that the other three don't want anything to do with him, so he's trying to charm Elliott. He's probably feeding him pizzas, burgers, cream cakes and anything he wants now."

"It's ok. It's ok. "Roger held her close. "I'll go round there and bash his brains out."

"Then you'll be up on a murder charge." She buried her head in his chest and closed her eyes. "I've got to be home by 6 o'clock."

"We've got some time left to cuddle before breakfast. Then we 'll have a nice shower and a stroll along the seafront and after lunch I'll drive you home."

"Thanks Roger. So sorry about all of this."

"It's ok. I'm having a lovely weekend. Forget it."

CHAPTER 36

JULIAN WOKE EARLY and wondered at what point he'd stopped thinking about Malcolm. Was it while the drum and bass had pounded through his ears at the club? Was it while he was making a fool of himself on the dance floor with Simon? Or was it much later back at the flat when Simon had said there was no need to crash on the sofa when he had a perfectly good double bed?

Julian lay awake as Simon slept, and pondered his good fortune. Little more than a day ago he was contemplating ending it all on the rails at London Bridge tube station. Now thanks to Simon's kindness and generosity he felt a whole lot better, albeit embarrassed and ashamed of his own actions that night.

Simon stirred and woke.

"Hey. You're still here then. You didn't chuck yourself over the Embankment!"

"No, you'd only jump in and pull me out. I'd have got wet for nothing." Julian was enjoying the banter.

"Do you want some coffee?" Simon stood up and pulled on some shorts.

"Sure. A bacon roll would go down well too."

"Don't want much do you?" "Give me all
your money as well."

"I haven't got any. I was going to sponge off you."

Julian smiled, but realised his weekend was coming to a close. He wasn't looking forward to leaving his new friend and catching the train back to Norfolk. Work beckoned, and Simon would soon be starting another shift at the hospital. He felt momentarily depressed at the thought of yet another day trying to satisfy the whims of ladies past their prime who were begging him to make them look 30 years younger in order to stop their husbands wandering.

"Why look so miserable?" Simon handed Julian a cup of coffee.

"Oh, just thinking about work tomorrow. I think I need a change."

"Give it some serious thought. What's keeping you up in Norfolk?"

"Malcolm was. Now he's gone I've got to move. I've just realised I can't afford to rent the flat on my own." Julian sighed and sipped his coffee.

"Where are your family?"

"Dad disowned me when I brought my first boyfriend home. I still see Mum though; they got divorced and she lives in Somerset with her new partner. I don't have any sis-ters or brothers."

Simon put his arm around Julian, sitting morosely on the edge of the bed:

"Hey. I'd be glad for you to stay here if you wanted to look for work in London. I'll ask at Guy's; they have quite a few hairdressers there that go around the wards prettying up the patients. Some of them really need prettying up as well. It could be a new start for you."

Julian felt the tears start to prick the back of his eyes:

"You're so kind, and I'm such a twat."

"Don't start that again. Catch your train, sort your life out, and let me know what's happening. You've got my mo-bile number, and you know where I am."

"Thanks so much for everything."

"Hey; it's not a problem."

Julian stood on the platform and watched the train come in that was to take him to Norwich and away from Simon. He imagined himself lying on the rails feeling the steel wheels run over his body. He looked away and shivered, but suddenly felt buoyed and excited for the future; he had found a new friend. It was early days yet, but he knew somehow that Simon was definitely going to be the one for him.

CHAPTER 37

ROZ SPRINTED UP the stairs to the Pilates room, but was disappointed to see a notice on the door saying the course had been cancelled due to lack of interest. On hearing a sound behind her she turned around to see Alice slowly climbing the stairs, straining her eyes to read the notice.

"It's cancelled. Lack of interest."

"Oh no! Just as I was getting into keeping fit."

"We can ask Ann at the desk to see if there's any other classes."

"Ok. I must shift some of this weight. My knees are starting to complain."

As they walked down the stairs Roz had an idea.

"Why don't you join the gym? I often nip in there for an hour or so while Jimmy's at school. They have personal trainers who work out the right exercise programme for you. It could be just what you need."

"Only if you go with me. I'm too nervous to go on my own."

"Sure. We can work out together. You'll soon be fitter than you'd ever thought possible."

"I doubt it, but it'll be a start anyway."

Roz waited at the desk while Alice signed up.

"When do you want to start? After we've dropped the kids off tomorrow? There's no time like the present."

"Oh, let me get my head round it first." "Tomorrow's good for me."

"Alright then, you win; tomorrow it is." Alice had a sudden thought. "Does the gym have a communal changing room? There's no way I'm changing in front of everybody else."

"It is communal, but there's a couple of cubicles." "Thank God for that."

"You're back early." Mark appeared in the hallway as Roz opened the front door.

"Pilates is no more. You're going to have to put up with me hanging around on a Monday evening."

"That's fine with me." He gave her a kiss. "I've just put Jimmy in bed. Do you want me to heat your dinner up? That chicken pie you made was lovely.

"I'll just go and see if he's still awake first. If you're heating it up, don't give me any pastry, just the chicken."

"All the more for me then."

Roz smiled; the compromise was working and her relationship with Mark seemed more harmonious these days. You could lead a man to tofu, but you couldn't make him eat it. However, Roz considered whether it was worth trying to slip in another healthy eating evening to see if she could get away with it.

"Hello Mummy. Can I have a story?"

"Of course you can, darling."

"They all wanted some of the cake in my lunch box today, but I told them it was mine."

"Mummy made it especially for you." "That's what I told them."

Give the people what they want. Roz couldn't understand how anybody would want to eat cake or pastry, but Mark was right; it was a free country. People put into their bodies what they wanted to. She even thought about frying them some fish and chips tomorrow, just as long as she didn't have to eat any of it.

CHAPTER 38

MIRIAM PETERS HELD her grand-daughter close in her arms. She could see that the baby's resemblance to Neville was remarkable.

"She didn't make a sound all through the ceremony, bless her!" Sylvia Frost stroked the baby-fine skin and wondered how soon she could prise little Georgina away from Miriam.

"Isn't she an absolute peach!" Miriam held the baby closer and turned away slightly to face the happy couple.

"Now we want the groom's mother, partner, sisters and husbands please." The photographer looked around, eager to hurry the guests before the rain began.

"I'll take the baby. You go and have your photo done."

With some reluctance Miriam handed over her precious bundle. Sylvia's face softened as she gazed down at her grand-daughter. She could see Georgina was the image of Thelma.

"Come on Mum. Come and stand next to me." Neville, holding his new bride's hand, smiled at his mother. "Stan, you're next to Mum, and then Donna and Denise can stand next to Thelma. Jack and Steve, can you stand behind them?

Neville had never felt so happy.   He was pushing 40, but

at last he had everything that he'd ever wanted; a beautiful wife and daughter, and enough money so that Thelma didn't have to work anymore.

"Can you kiss your bride for me Neville?"

The photographer snapped away as Neville was happy to oblige. He'd never been kissed so much as he had been in the past year. Thelma's passion knew no bounds, and instead of reading himself to sleep as he used to do, on most nights he was now intertwined with the love of his life and breath-less with exertion.

"Now can we have just the bride, groom and baby please."

Thelma smoothed down imaginary creases in her ivory silk dress as she took her daughter from her mother.

"I've only held her for five minutes. She's had her for ag-es." Sylvia indicated towards Miriam, who was making her way over to them again.

"Don't worry. I'll give her straight back to you in a mi-nute."

Thelma couldn't wait to give the baby back, and couldn't un-derstand why their mothers were making so much fuss about Georgina. The baby's screams when she was awake were enough to wake the dead. How Neville was managing to sleep through it every night she couldn't quite fathom; some nights she had the sneaky feeling he was feigning sleep and was actually just as wide awake as she was. She sighed; her life had spiralled out of control. One careless action had cost her dearly; her independence, her job, and maybe was now even encroaching upon her sanity. The only things to look forward to every day were sex (provided the baby didn't wake up and spoil it) and pinot grigio. The latter dulled her senses to a comfortably numb level, just enough for her to cope with the daily monotonous routine.

She looked down at her daughter, sleeping peacefully in her arms; shitty nappies, screaming, making up bottles, feed-ing, and then more shit. This was motherhood?

She walked back to Neville, carrying the baby. She smiled at him and could see he was almost bursting with pride and happiness. She wished they could have had a few years alone together before becoming parents, but as much as she wanted to she could hardly send Georgina back to where she came from (she suddenly had a mental picture of shoving the baby back up into her womb to silence the screams).

"Come on darling. Let's get a photo of the three of us before Georgina tells us she's hungry."

Neville put his arm around his wife's shoulders; he was surprised she didn't look happier. Wasn't a bride supposed to be radiant on her wedding day? The only time he ever saw her happy these days was while they were having sex, or after drinking a couple of glasses of wine in the evenings.

The photographer came to the conclusion that the bride had probably never smiled in her life. Thelma grimaced for the photographer and then gave the baby back to her mother, who cooed and fussed over her like somebody demented. Thelma felt a stab of annoyance; why couldn't she feel the same way that her mother did about her own daughter? What was wrong with her?

"Now can we have the bride's family please?"

Miriam walked across the grass to where Sylvia was standing with Georgina.

"I'll take her now; it's time for your photo."

"I'll take her with me. After all, she's part of the bride's family!"

Sylvia held her head high as she walked carefully with her grand-daughter to join the wedding group. That woman was not going to get her hands on the baby for any longer than was necessary if she could help it. What if Georgina started to prefer Miriam to her? That would never do!

CHAPTER 39

ROGER WAS HAPPY to have got Judy off the council estate. It hadn't been the best place to live, but now with the money from the sale of his flat he'd been able to put a sizeable deposit down on a semi in a more upmarket street nearby, so that Elliot and Marlon could still go to the same school. He was seemingly getting along well with Judy's three eldest boys who had accepted his presence in their lives, but the youngest boy was proving to be somewhat of a problem.

Elliott hated him with a vengeance. Roger had no intention of trying to take the place of his father, but it would have been a nice start for the boy to give him a civil 'good morning' at breakfast instead of the usual grunt, especially as Roger reasoned it was now mostly his own money putting food on the table. Judy always said he'd come around in time, but most days Roger felt like shaking the boy to get some sort of reaction out of him.

"Morning, Elliott."

"Mmm."

"Do you want a lift to school this morning?" Silence.

"Can I have a lift please Roger?" Marlon finished his third slice of toast in as many minutes. "I've got Maths GCSE today."

"Sure. I'll be leaving in about half an hour."

"Aren't you coming with us Elliott?" Marlon looked towards his brother as Elliott stood up from the table.

"I'm leaving now. I'm walking. Bye Mum."

"See you later. Have a good day." For the sake of peace Judy decided it was better to turn a blind eye to her youngest son's behaviour.

"What is it with that boy? I can't do a thing right except give him pocket money." Roger dried the dishes as Judy washed.

"He misses his father and he's at that funny age. He doesn't realise what a shit-bag Alan actually is. He always looked up to him. The other three can see him for what he really is."

"Oh well, I'll keep trying. It's all I can do apart from murdering him."

"But then I won't speak to you."

"Life's a bitch." Roger gave Judy a quick kiss. "Have you seen my keys? I'd better be off."

"They're on the table in the hallway."

"Come on Marlon! See you later Jude."

As Roger drove nearer to the school he could see Elliott up ahead of him. The boy was walking as fast as he could with his head down. There were two older boys following him rather too closely, one on either side.

"That's Carl Stickland and his brother. They're arseholes. We'll have to give him a bit of help, Rog."

"No problem."

Roger seized his chance. After quickly parking the car he and Marlon soon caught up with Elliott, whose face rapidly tried to hide a smile of relief.

"Ok Elliott?" Roger looked over his shoulder as the Stickland brothers scowled and started to hang back.

"Yeah, thanks Roger. Thanks Marlon. They were hassling me. They want money."

"What's the point of asking you? You've never got any!" Marlon laughed and the two boys waved to Roger as they disappeared through the school gates.

As Roger turned the key in the lock that evening he was surprised to be greeted by a less-than-surly Elliott:

"Hi Roger."

"How's it going, Elliott?"

"All right I suppose."

"Did those boys trouble you again?"

"Nah. They moved on to hassle somebody else."

"Just let me know if they bother you again."

"Ok. Thanks."

Roger decided to push his luck.

"Fancy a trip to see the game on Saturday? I've got a couple of tickets to see Norwich play." Roger knew Terry at work would be gutted not to be accompanying him, but family must come first.

"Great! Thanks Roger!" Elliott ran upstairs to tell Marlon the good news.

"What was that all about?" Judy was setting the table for dinner and had only kept half an ear on the conversation.

"Oh, nothing much." Roger gave her a kiss. "Just boy stuff."

"There's too many boys around here. It's time we had some girls."

"Give them a while. They're all working on that I'm sure."

CHAPTER 40

THE WARD MANAGER had asked him to visit Mrs Taylor; she must be a new patient. As he made his way to ward 8 with his hairdryer and trays of curlers, Julian wondered if what Simon had told him was true; that the old ladies loved him. He hadn't been aware that his presence was bringing untold comfort to the elderly, but a steady flow of female patients well past their prime that visited his little salon in the hospital foyer had seemed to reinforce the message.

Opening the outer doors to the ward, Julian wrinkled his nose as the smell of excreta assailed his nostrils. He didn't know how Simon could enjoy working in such a fetid atmosphere. He preferred to be downstairs in his salon as much as he could, dressing the hair of the walking wounded. However, calls such as these from the ward manager couldn't be ignored.

"Hi Julian." Tina the Ward Clerk looked up from sorting piles of notes. "She's in the end bay. First bed on the left."

As Julian rolled his trays up to the bedside he almost gasped at the sight of the old lady. She had been ravaged by some unknown disease and now possibly could only weigh about five stones at the most. Her skin was yellow and had the consistency of parchment, and her eyes were sunk back into her head. Her hair was sparse and stood up in wisps on her scalp.

"Hello. I'm Violet, darling." Her voice came out as a whisper. "I'm dying, but hey, don't we all in the end."

As she struggled to sit up the bright blue eyes staring out at him from a tiny, wizened face unnerved Julian. He put on his best forced smile and wondered what on earth he could do to improve her appearance.

"Can you make me look a bit smarter, darling? My son's coming to visit this afternoon. I don't want him to see me looking like this."

"We'll soon have you shipshape. Shall I give your hair a little wash?" Julian wondered how much of it would be left by the time he'd finished. He would need to be extra careful.

"Maybe just dampen it down, put it in rollers and give it a little blow-dry? I can't get out of bed to have it washed properly you see." The effort of speaking so many words at once was causing Violet to become breathless. Her breath came in noisy rasps.

"Don't you worry Violet; your son will see just what a beautiful mother he has."

"You've got the gift of the gab, you have. Hey I don't suppose you've got a cigarette on you by any chance? Violet puffed and panted as she looked hopefully at Julian.

"Don't even think about it Violet." Julian set out his trays, looked at Violet, and wondered if he should work a bit harder at giving up smoking.

"It was worth a try."

Julian took Violet's wash sponge, dampened down her hair, and used his small curlers to carefully roll up what was left of Violet's tresses. Some of it came away in his hands, and he hurriedly tossed it in the bin and hoped she didn't see. He put the blow-dryer on the coolest setting and hoped for the best.

"There! That's better! You're ready for the ball now, Violet!"

"No, I'm ready for my coffin darling, but I've lived a full

and happy life and I'm not afraid of death."

The old lady was tired, but she smiled up at him and Julian felt tears spring to his eyes. He busied himself putting away the rollers and hoped he wouldn't break down before he got out of the ward.

"You take care of yourself Violet. Call me again if you need another hairdo."

"I'll be fine now. Thank you." Violet leaned back against the pillows and sighed.

Julian arrived back at the salon and left the closed sign on the door for a few minutes while he let the tears fall. Violet would never see the outside world again, but he'd learned a valuable lesson from that frail old lady; enjoy life and live it to the full. There'd be no more bollocks about jumping in front of trains; with Simon by his side he was going to give up drinking and smoking and live a long and happy life until the Grim Reaper insisted it was time for him to go.

CHAPTER 41

ALICE SMILED AS she zipped up her skirt. She'd managed to lose exactly seven stones in a year, and she felt like a new person. Her long auburn hair shone with health, and her skin was clear and radiant. She twirled a little pirouette in front of the mirror as her daughter clapped and cheered. With their new diet regime Lucy had also lost several pounds, and was no longer being teased at school about her weight.

"Come on, we're going round to see Auntie Roz."

"Yeah! Jimmy's got a new bike. He's going to let me have a go on it."

Alice could hear raised voices inside as she rang the doorbell. Roz took longer than usual to answer, and as soon as Alice saw her she knew what had happened. Alice noticed Mark giving her a wink as he passed her on his way out of the front door, carrying a large holdall. She pretended not to notice.

"You ok?" Alice was concerned for her friend. It was unusual for Roz to be anything other than cool, calm and collected.

"Fine. Come in. Jimmy's been waiting for Lucy to come over."

The children went off to play in the garden. Alice seated herself at the kitchen table and Roz switched the kettle on.

"He's leaving me, Alice. Mark's got another woman, but he hasn't told me who she is. He's found somebody else though." She gave a rueful laugh. "She's probably lured him in with her deep fat fryer." Admitting what she had suspected for some time caused further tears to run down her cheeks.

"Surely not? You two have been together for years!" Al-ice tried to sound as surprised as she could.

Roz stirred her coffee morosely and looked down into her cup.

"He confirmed last night that he's been seeing somebody else. I've got to let Jimmy know somehow that his daddy's leaving. He'll be devastated; he worships the ground Mark walks on."

Alice felt like bursting into tears along with her friend. She had been so wrapped up in herself. With Roz's support and encouragement she had lost a whole seven stones. The resulting boost in self-confidence and change in her appearance had made men smile as they took second glances.

Mark had taken a second glance that first time he had come home late from work to pick Jimmy up while Roz had been at one of her exercise classes. Alice could see it in his eyes; she had been flattered with the knowledge that he'd found her attractive. No man had looked at her since Lucy's birth, and she was ashamed to admit that she'd flirted with him just a tiny bit. After that night it had always been Mark who would pick up Jimmy, and she always looked forward to his mildly sexual banter. However, when Jimmy was at home with Roz and Mark had turned up at her flat on the night he was supposed to be visiting his mother, she knew it was wrong but she'd let him in.

Their sexual chemistry was almost palpable. Alice hadn't even waited to ensure Lucy was asleep; they'd had sex almost straight away on the sofa, the act itself bringing a relief of the tension between them, but also new feelings of guilt and betrayal. There had been many other times since then, but she never thought Mark would have ever left Roz; he hadn't even told her he loved her. She wasn't even sure if she did have any deep feelings for Mark; all she knew was that she had enjoyed the attention and the sex.

"Can't you try again, for Jimmy's sake?" The thought of a little boy without the father he adored was too much. She'd been so concerned with herself that she hadn't even thought about Jimmy. She decided there and then that she could never see Mark again.

"No, it's too late. He's had sex with somebody else. It's spoilt our relationship and I can never trust him again."

"Oh, Roz. I'm so sorry." Alice felt like bawling her eyes out. At that moment she wanted the ground to open up and swallow her whole.

"Hey, it's not your fault! It just goes to show the type of man he is. I don't know how many women he's had; he's done it once and he'll do it again to someone else. He's not to be trusted. He's taken all his stuff now anyway. He won't be coming back."

"If you want me to look after Jimmy so that you two can sort things out, I'm quite willing."

"Thanks Alice." Roz sniffed. "There's no need."

A depression settled over Alice when she returned to the flat with Lucy. She knew it was just a matter of time before Mark rang the doorbell, looking for a place to stay. However, nobody rang the bell that evening or the next. Alice checked with Roz, but Mark had not returned. She felt less guilty when she could truthfully tell her friend that she hadn't seen him about either.

After a month had gone past with no sign of Mark, Alice came to the conclusion that he had indeed found another woman. She was filled with the greatest relief that the woman was not herself, and that her friendship with Roz had re-mained undamaged. She would take more care next time.

"D'you fancy going back to the leisure centre? I think there's a new Pilates class starting on Thursday evenings."

Alice stood with Lucy and Roz at the school gates while they waited for Jimmy to fetch his bicycle.

"Maybe. I'll see if Mum can babysit first." Roz waved to Jimmy over at the other end of the playground, and Alice thought she seemed a little bit happier of late.

CHAPTER 42

NEVILLE COULD HEAR the baby screaming as he turned the key in the lock.

"Hi Thelma!"

He put his laptop case down in the hallway and ran upstairs. His daughter was alone in her bedroom, standing up and gripping the sides of her cot, with tears pouring down her face.

"It's ok. It's ok. Daddy's home now." Neville picked up the sodden toddler and changed her nappy. Her cries subsided with the attention, and she sucked her thumb.

"Let's go and find Mummy." He carried the baby downstairs and looked in the kitchen. There was no sign of Thelma.

"Thelma!" He called out as he walked into the living room.

Oh no, not again!

The empty bottle of wine on the floor near to her hand said it all, as Neville walked over to the sofa to where Thelma lay sleeping off its effects. Another half empty bottle stood on the coffee table nearby, next to a dirty nappy and an unwashed plate containing the remains of a mashed banana.

"Thelma!"

He tried to shake her awake, but his efforts only met with loud snoring. Neville gave up, made himself a sandwich, fed and washed the baby, and spent the evening playing with his daughter who gurgled away happily as soon all her needs had been satisfied.

It was nearly nine o'clock when Thelma awoke to find Neville looking at her from the armchair opposite. Her head throbbed, and she felt disorientated and sick.

"Where's Georgina?" She sat up slowly.

"You were drunk yet again, and left her in her cot to scream. I've fed her, given her a bath, and put her to bed. She's asleep now, no thanks to you."

"Oh God, I'm sorry. I'm so sorry." Thelma rubbed her eyes and struggled to adjust to reality.

"You have to get help. I can't trust you with our daughter any more. I'm going to have to turn down work in order to stay here now and look after Georgina. You're fucking useless. You're an alcoholic and I'm sick of coming home and finding you like this."

Neville had never felt so angry in his life. Hadn't he given Thelma everything a woman could ever want? They had a huge four-bedroom detached house in a desirable area; he earned a good salary which provided the means for expensive holidays and days out, yet she had hardly smiled since the baby had been born 18 months ago. He was at his wits' end.

Thelma stood up and felt her stomach retch and heave, ready to expel its contents. Making her way unsteadily to the downstairs toilet she vomited back the pinot grigio and the baby's leftover banana and felt a bit better. After rinsing her mouth at the sink she looked up to see Neville's face in the mirror. She turned around.

"I'm not an alcoholic Neville, I'm just unhappy. You don't realise what's it's like here every day. You go out to see customers and I'm just left with screaming. The baby doesn't like me. I can't do anything right." She wiped her mouth on a fluffy white towel and looked at her husband.

"Of course she likes you! You're her mother for Christ's

sake! Think of her instead of thinking of yourself for once!"

"I do, but I can't cope with the screaming and the tantrums. I used to have a responsible job; I was a librarian. Now look at me; I can't even look after a baby properly, and look at my body." Thelma dissolved into tears and wished she could walk out the front door and keep going until she found peace and quiet.

"What's wrong with your body? I love your body!"

"I'm out of condition. I used to have good abdominal muscles. Now I look like a sack of potatoes."

Neville put his arms around his wife and sighed.

"What do you want? What can I give you?" Thelma rested her head on her husband's shoulder.

"My freedom. I need to go out to work. I want to join an exercise class again. I'm not cut out for motherhood. I'm useless at it. I've had to give up my job and I'm desperately unhappy. Can't you see?"

"Then we'll get a nanny. Is that what you want?" "Yes. It's what I want."

"Shall we ask one of our mothers if they'd like the job?"

"No; definitely not. I don't want your mother poking her nose about in here, and my mother's not fit enough."

"I'll leave it to you to organise one then. Join an exercise class in the evenings and I'll look after Georgina. However, the next time I see you drunk and incapable I'll be informing Social Services."

"You bastard."

"You'd better make sure there's not a next time then."

"There won't be, I promise." "That's what you said last time."

Neville disentangled himself, went upstairs and got into bed in the spare room. He heard Thelma come into the room after her shower, but he pretended to be asleep. He heard her tiptoe out and close the door.

CHAPTER 43

"CAN WE STOP at the library, Rog? I need to get some books out for my school project."

"Sure."

Roger felt in a good mood. His team had won that afternoon, and his relationship with Elliott had definitely taken an upward turn; the boy now hung around him like a shadow. He parked the car and followed Elliott into the library's foyer. It had recently been refurbished and extended, and Roger looked around appreciatively.

"Where can I find books on the Tudors please?"

Elliott spoke to somebody behind a computer desk, and Roger thought the woman looked as if she had never smiled in her entire life. He thought he recognised her from somewhere, but he couldn't for the life of him remember where it was.

"Over there in the history section." Elliot followed the direction of the woman's finger as she pointed to a corner opposite.

"Haven't I seen you somewhere before?" Roger had noticed a flicker of recognition in the woman's thin features.

"I think it was at the Pilates class last year." Thelma had recognised the uncouth builder straight away.

"Course it was! Do you still go?"

"It closed, but I think there's a new class starting again on

Thursday evenings." Thelma sniffed and looked back at her computer, hoping the ghastly fat man would go away.

"I'll let Judy know. Cheers, darling." Roger noticed her wedding ring and wondered why anybody in their right mind would have wanted to marry her.

I'm not your darling!

Thelma looked up from her computer, relieved that the builder had disappeared. He'd distracted her from her people-watching; she liked to watch the mothers and toddlers these days. She liked to imagine the day when she could bring Georgina into the library and they could look at a book together without her daughter flying into a tantrum and pulling all the books off the shelves.

Had she given birth to an alien? Thelma didn't know. All she did know was that Georgina had a terrible temper if she didn't get exactly what she wanted. Neville and the nanny Katrina could handle her screams, but Thelma always dissolved into a useless wreck at the first sign of her daughter's frequent mood changes. She was sure Georgina was picking up on it and turning her mother's inability to cope to her own advantage, and this made Thelma feel even more useless and unhappy.

Out of the corner of her eye she saw the builder and what looked like his son reappear with an armful of books each. The boy obviously loved his father, and she watched them talking to each other and smiling as they waited in the queue to be served. She felt a wave of jealousy overcome her; she felt no connection to her daughter! What was the matter with her? Every morning she couldn't wait to get out of the house - was this normal? Was she normal?

Thelma watched the builder and his son walk out of the main doors. She sighed and realised that in a short while she would have to make her way home. Katrina would have cooked something and would be feeding Georgina, who would be positively beaming at her nanny and her father as they laughed together over the baby's efforts to feed herself. Thelma felt in the way in her own house, useless and second-rate compared to Katrina's superior child-rearing skills and prowess in the kitchen. Was Katrina thinking about moving in with Neville and taking Georgina away from her? The three of them seemed like a perfect family. Thelma felt tears prick the back of her eyes. She felt like drinking a whole bottle of wine to dull the reality, but then she remembered Neville's threat to inform Social Services.

Roger unlocked the front door and smiled as Elliott bounded into the kitchen to find his mother.

"We won today, Mum!"

Judy could hardly believe the change for the better in her youngest son. Elliott was thriving; even his own father wasn't showing him the same support and guidance as Roger. The boy had even lost some weight, and his self-confidence was growing. He and Roger had found a common interest in football, and although Judy didn't care two hoots whether Norwich won or not, she relished the few hours' peace and quiet every other Saturday afternoon to do her own thing while they were at the game.

"Hey, that's great!" She lifted her face to Roger's for a kiss.

"Roger bought me a Norwich shirt! Look!" Elliott held up his new prized acquisition."

"That's mine, dickhead." Marlon suddenly appeared from the depths of his room, helped himself to a steaming potato from the colander with one hand, and snatched the shirt away with the other.

"Roger – he's got my shirt!"

"Marlon, behave yourself. You don't even like football!" Roger laughed at the thought of Marlon wanting to watch a football match.

"Give it back or you won't get any dinner. I'm putting one less plate out now." Judy kept a straight face and removed Marlon's knife and fork from the table.

"Ok. I don't want it that bad." Marlon threw the shirt back to his brother, retrieved his knife and fork, and sat down at the dinner table.

"Who's joining us for dinner today?" Roger hoped all the family would be there to hear his news.

"Brian should be back any minute. He and Lewis are at the pub. Lewis is here for dinner as well."

"Yes I know; I asked him." Roger wanted his son to be there when he sprang his surprise.

"Nick's round Babs' place."

"Babs? Who's Babs?"

"The latest conquest. He's working his way through all the females in the local vicinity."

"Good God. I hope he doesn't catch a nasty little rash."

Roger waited until all the family (with the exception of Nick) were seated. He felt nervous, but excited all at the same time.

"Judy; keep the food warm for a minute. I've got something to say first."

He felt everyone's eyes upon him, including Judy's. He knew she had no idea what was coming.

"As you know, Judy and I have been together for some time now. You've all accepted me into your home and I've been happier recently than I've been for ages." He looked towards Judy and smiled. She returned his smile with a quizzical look.

"What's up?" Brian could sense something was coming around the corner, and he wanted to find out what it was.

"Yeah Dad. Spit it out." Lewis was as keen as Brian to find out what was going on.

"Well, Lewis, how do you fancy a new step-mother?" "What?"

"What I'm trying to say is – Judy, will you marry me?"

Roger produced a small box from his pocket, opened it and gave it to Judy who looked at the engagement ring incredulously.

Elliott looked to Roger and then back again to his mother. "Wow! What do you say Mum?"

Judy's eyes filled with tears as she held the box. Roger would make a reliable, dependable husband. They could grow old together. He made her laugh.

"I'll say yes, Roger. Yes, I'll marry you."

All four boys clapped and cheered. Judy cried, and Roger let out a huge sigh of relief as he placed the ring on the third finger of Judy's left hand.

"I love you Jude."

"I love you too."

"Can we have some dinner now?"

Marlon was hungry. He'd waited long enough.

CHAPTER 44

SHE'D PERFECTED THE art of drinking vodka in the car before starting work at the library. There was no tell-tale smell on her breath for Neville to find in the evenings, and the alcohol put her in a comfortable frame of mind at the start of the day and took away the pain of knowing that her daughter was happier being looked after by another woman.

Thelma stopped the car a couple of streets away from the library, reached down under the driver's seat and brought out a half-bottle of the clear nectar. Gulping down a few more mouthfuls she closed her eyes and felt the alcohol warm her body. However, more recently she was finding that she often craved its effects later on in the day as well and was starting to give in to temptation, but had not let Neville anywhere near her on those evenings in case he suspected something.

Arriving at the library she stashed the bottle back under the driver's seat before turning off the engine. She wondered how on earth she'd got through the days without it before. Her job was easier to bear with a snifter or two under her belt, and even the besotted mothers cooing over their toddlers didn't bother her half as much.

Monica watched her boss walking across the car park. Mrs Peters seemed different these days; more relaxed and less uptight. She was less short-tempered, but often seemed distant and in a world of her own. She wasn't sure why the change had happened, but wondered if her colleagues were right when they whispered to her under their breath that alcohol was the cause. Monica wasn't the sort of person to judge or speak badly about anybody, and she found the slurs on her boss's character hard to bear.

"Good morning Monica!" Thelma's smile was radiant.

"Morning Mrs Peters." Monica was unsure, but thought she could smell a whiff of alcohol as her boss walked by.

"I'll be with you in a moment; just need to hang up my coat." Thelma walked to the cloakroom and Monica followed with her eyes.

"I bet she's pissed already; can't you smell the vodka? I know a lush when I see one!" Caroline the children's librarian smiled conspiratorially at Monica as she gathered up the late returned items from the previous day.

"Do you think so?" Monica wondered if Caroline was telling the truth.

"Absolutely. I bet she's hiding bottles of the stuff in her locker."

"Why does she need to drink?" Monica followed Caroline around to the bookshelves.

"'Cos she's a lush; I just told you!" "Perhaps she's unhappy."

"Who cares? She's always been unhappy. Even if she won a million pounds on the lottery I bet her face still wouldn't crack a smile." Caroline placed a returned novel back on the shelf and tidied the surrounding books.

"You can open up the main doors now, Monica." Thelma emerged from the ladies' cloakroom and sighed at the thought of the long day ahead. She sat at her desk and wondered if she would be missing Georgina speaking her first words. She imagined Katrina laughing and cuddling the baby, and jealousy tore like a knife through her body. Georgina naturally went first to Katrina now, and as she took a quick sip from the bottle of vodka in her handbag Thelma wondered if her daughter now thought of Katrina as her mother.

By the end of the working day quite a few more sips had managed to dull the pain. Thelma walked back to her car in a happier frame of mind. She started the engine, pulled out of the car park and onto the dual carriageway, imagining all the while how her daughter's face might light up with pleasure at the sight of her mother returning home after a hard day's toil. Her daughter's features were exquisite; Thelma momentarily closed her eyes to augment the mental image. As it transpired, her baby's face turned out to be the last thing that she ever thought about on the earthly plane.

CHAPTER 45

"I FEEL A right tart in this getup." Roger made a slight adjustment to the over-tight cravat. "Look at it; it's pink for Christ's sake."

"Yeah. You actually look like a right tart as well." Brian grinned at his new stepfather, "I think I even fancy you myself."

"Well, you look like a bloody pimp." Roger sleeked back his hair in the mirror and looked at the reflection of his stepson.

"This stuff's making it smell like a tart's boudoir in here anyway." Brian checked the label on the liquid soap as he washed his hands. "Are you happy it's all over now Rog?"

Roger checked his flies and buttoned up his jacket.

"Yeah, I am. It was a bit nerve-wracking standing before that registrar, I can tell you. You wait until it's your turn."

"Give over. You won't get me agreeing to keep some bird for life."

"That's what I used to say when I was your age. Now look at me; this is the second time I've waltzed up the aisle."

"Mum's as happy as a pig in shit. You must be doing something right."

"Cheers. We just seemed to click. You'll know when you've found the right girl."

The door to the men's toilet opened and Elliott's head appeared.

"Mum sent me to find you two; the food's ready now."

"We're just coming." Roger held open the door for Brian to walk through.

"El, d'you know what?" Brian looked at his youngest brother who was dressed in a dark suit that seemed slightly too large for his recently slimmed-down frame.

"What?"

"You definitely look like an undertaker."

As Elliott's arm lifted to punch Brian, he screamed as he suddenly found himself encased in a headlock.

"Don't even think about it, little brother." Brian's biceps twitched under his tail coat.

"Don't damage that suit. It's got to go back on Monday." Roger extricated Elliot's neck from his brother's grip.

"All he needs is a hearse to walk in front of and he's laughing." Brian ruffled his brother's hair as they walked towards the banqueting hall.

Roger gazed at Judy; he'd never seen her looking so beautiful. Her womanly figure had been shown off to its best advantage in that clinging long silky creation (God knows how much it had cost), and her happiness radiated out for all to see. He swallowed; he seemed to have a catch in his throat. He smiled over at his new bride sitting at the top table, who was in the process of receiving gifts and cards from family and friends. He thought he was just about the luckiest bugger in the whole wide world.

"Look Rog: my auntie Glad has given us £500!"

"Well, that'll pay the outstanding balance on your dress." "Cheeky sod. It didn't cost that much."

Roger sat down beside Judy and gave her hand a squeeze. "Happy?"

"Of course I am. It's my wedding day. Why wouldn't I be?"

The waiters approached with the first course, and Roger looked appreciatively at the pate and toast he'd ordered.

"Make the most of it; after our honeymoon it's going to be pilchards and Pilates. We've got to get back to keeping fit again."

"Oh, bloody hell."

CHAPTER 46

"WE COMMEND HER body to the ground; earth to earth, ashes to ashes, and dust to dust. In sure and certain hope of the resurrection to eternal life."

Neville stood in a daze by the graveside; hardly hearing a word the vicar was speaking. He wasn't sure or certain of anything.

Was his wife really dead? Had she really drunkenly driven into a lamppost and fractured her skull? Did he really have a daughter? Where was she? Surely this was just a bad dream and he would soon be waking up next to Thelma, the love of his life. They would laugh about it, and Thelma would kiss his fears away.....

Eyes swimming with tears, he looked around for his daughter. Miriam Peters took her son's hand and gave it a comforting squeeze.

He had no idea what to say to the myriad of relatives who gathered in his kitchen after the funeral service. He held his baby close in his old comfortable armchair; Georgina seemed to sense something was wrong and sat quietly on her father's lap, sucking her thumb. Once or twice she held out her arms to her nanny, but Katrina was busy making sandwiches and tea, thinking it best to keep in the background.

"Will you keep Katrina on to look after Georgina?" Miriam tried to pull her son out of his reverie.

"Of course. Georgie loves her." Neville knew the love was reciprocal. His baby would be well cared for. He felt his eyes fill with tears again.

"Well if there's anything I can do to help, just let me know."

"And me. I'm only too willing to help." Sylvia Frost's arms ached to hold her daughter's child.

"Thanks, but we'll be fine."

Neville put his head down and smelt his daughter's clean baby hair. He wished everybody would go home. He just wanted to be alone with Georgina and think about the good times he'd had with Thelma.

It seemed an eternity, but one by one the guests left. Neville put his daughter in her high chair and gave her some ham sandwiches to eat and filled her baby cup with milk from the fridge.

"I've washed up and put everything away Mr Peters. I expect you'll be taking a few days off work now?" Katrina put on her jacket and picked up her car keys.

"No. Come back tomorrow. I need to work to take my mind off everything." Neville searched around on his desk and gave her a small brown envelope.

"Here's last week's wages. Sorry they're late. Thank you for all your help today."

"No problem. I'll see you tomorrow." Katrina thought it best to go and let him grieve in peace.

When he heard the front door close Neville looked at his motherless daughter eating contentedly, and wept.

CHAPTER 47

PETRA BOUNDED UP the stairs to the Pilates room and opened the door. She hoped the new course would fare better than the previous one. The room was full, and surprisingly there seemed to be a few familiar faces.

"Hi everyone. Welcome to the first class. I'm Petra. Has anybody done Pilates with gym balls before?"

Five hands shot up in the air. Petra recognised the exercise freak and the ghastly builder straight away. A voice called out from the back.

"Hi Petra. Remember me? I'm Malcolm."

Ah yes, the gay one.

"Hi Malcolm. Who's that with you?"

"Rick. He hasn't done this before."

Petra couldn't for the life of her remember the name of Malcolm's previous friend.

"Hi Rick. Is the other chap coming as well?"

"No, Julian lives in London now, but I still see him sometimes." Malcolm had made his peace with Julian and was happy that he seemed settled with Simon.

"Ah, I see. Well, welcome Rick, and I hope you find the course interesting."

"Hi Petra. I'm Alice. I don't think you remember me? I've lost seven and a half stone in weight."

Petra looked towards the slim, lithe red-haired woman sitting on a gym ball next to the exercise freak (what on earth was that one's name again?). She didn't recognise her or remember her at all.

"Well done! That's a great achievement." Petra vaguely remembered a huge whale-like creature joining at the end of the previous course, but she wasn't sure if this woman could be one and the same.

"I'm sitting on my ball…s, Petra."

Judy giggled as her husband broke the ice in the only way he knew how. Petra sighed as a general tittering echoed around the room.

"Good for you Roger (she couldn't forget that one). I'll show you what you can do with them in a minute."

She turned on the portable CD player, and the thin reedy notes of an oboe rose above the sound of waves crashing onto the shore.

"I'll look forward to that, then."

EPILOGUE

THEY HAD PERFECTED a routine; Katrina would arrive at 8.30 on weekday mornings, and by then Neville would have fed and washed the baby and himself. Katrina would then clear away the breakfast things and take over Georgina's care while Neville went off to visit customers or work in his study. He found he could trundle through the day on autopilot; filling the hours quoting for life insurance, setting up trust funds, or working out tax returns. When he worked at his desk a photo of Thelma holding Georgina was never far away, and sometimes it seemed unreal to him that his wife was no longer alive.

After six months had passed, Katrina started to prepare his evening meal before she left in the afternoons. She had informed him the baby always needed feeding before he'd finished work, and that it was no trouble to cook one extra dinner. Neville wondered if she was hungry at that time herself, and suggested the idea that she could cook for all three of them for extra pay. Katrina had readily agreed, and so it was that every weekday around 5.30 in the afternoon the three of them would sit down to dinner. Neville found he didn't want to work past 5pm, as he had begun to look forward to sitting at the table and talking to Katrina to find out what his daughter had been up to all day.

At the weekends he had Georgina all to himself. He

would take her to the beach if the weather was good, or if it was raining to an indoor play area or to visit either of her grandmothers. He preferred to be out of the house, hating the silent rooms which had once been so full of Thelma's presence. He began to enjoy his little girl's company, and she blossomed under his guidance and attention.

As time went on he also realised that he was looking at Thelma's photo less, and was beginning to enjoy Katrina's company more. Her upbeat personality and even temper sat well with him, and she cared for his daughter with unflappable good humour. He was mindful to always keep the relationship on a professional level, as he was well aware of the large age gap between them, the fact that Katrina would probably already have a boyfriend, and also the stumbling block that she'd given no indication that she thought about him as anything other than an employer.

One Friday evening he turned off his computer at 4.55pm. The weekend stretched ahead without Katrina's laughter. Opening the door to his study he went along the hallway to the kitchen, where the agreeable aroma of beef stew and dumplings assailed his nostrils. Katrina was stirring the saucepan of stew with one hand, and balancing his daughter on her hip with the other.

"Daddy!" Georgina held her arms out to Neville, who took her from Katrina and gave her a cuddle.

"Hello my little princess." He whirled her around in the air and kissed her.

"Dinner's ready Mr Peters. Can you put Georgina in her seat, please?"

"Do call me Neville. Mr Peters sounds so stuffy."

"Ok, Neville. The dinner's still ready though." Katrina smiled and ladled the stew onto two large plates and one smaller plate.

"That's great. Thanks very much." Neville cut Georgina's dinner into manageable pieces and gave her a spoon.

"She almost said my name today; she called me Trina."

"She's growing up fast. My little princess will soon be

three." Neville smiled fondly over at his daughter, who returned his smile through a mouthful of mashed potato.

"I think I'll take Georgie to the Peppa Pig show at the Corn Exchange on Sunday afternoon."

"Oh, she'll love that. I'd love to see her face when she sees the puppets. It's her favourite TV show." Katrina picked up a teaspoon to help Georgina as Neville took a deep breath.

"If you're free, why don't you come along and you can see her face for yourself? The treat is on me."

"I'd love to. Thanks for asking me."

"No problem." Neville remembered to breathe out again. "We can all have dinner somewhere afterwards."

"Great. I'll look forward to it."

Neville found himself humming a tune as he answered the doorbell after Sunday lunch. Katrina smiled at him as she stood on the doorstep dressed in a white jumper, jeans, and a soft leather jacket. He thought she looked good enough to eat.

Katrina wondered if the day had finally arrived when Neville realised she existed. She had taken much time and trouble with her clothes and makeup, and she could tell her enhanced appearance had not gone unnoticed. She beamed a smile big enough to light up the sky; all in all she had always preferred older men.

The End

If you have enjoyed this story, you may wish to check out 'No Sex Please, I'm Menopausal!', a humorous novel also by Stevie Turner.

OTHER WORKS BY STEVIE TURNER

A House Without Windows
Lily: A Short Story
No Sex Please, I'm Menopausal!
For the Sake of a Child
A Rather Unusual Romance
The Daughter-in-law Syndrome
Revenge
The Noise Effect
The Donor
Repent at Leisure
Life: 18 Short Stories
Waiting in the Wings
Mind Games
A Marriage of Convenience
Leg-less and Chalaza: A dark novelette

9 781999 330378